DESIGNER BABIES

Volume Three

Passing the Torch

David Witt

Fat Chance Publishing

DESIGNER BABIES VOLUME THREE PASSING THE TORCH

ISBN 978-1-7342023-6-6

FIRST EDITION

Cover Design by Matt Witt

Attributions:

"Vecteezy.com"

"Designed by vectorstock (Image #25179632 at VectorStock.com)"

"Photo by rezasaad رضاصاد on Unsplash

To Karen, my awesome and lovely wife without who's unending support this novel would not have been possible. From reading rough drafts to suggesting ways to publicize my work, she was an important part of bringing this book to market. She has been a constant source of encouragement throughout our life journey together, and I can't wait for our next adventure!

Special thanks to the Thursday writer's group who welcomed me with open arms and honest feedback. You offered me an education and a sense of community for which I am grateful. I am so glad we went online and continued in a virtual format in the face of the pandemic.

It is also important that I thank Morgan Williams for his perspective and editing. I admire his ability to take a good scene and point out ways that I can make it better.

Sincere thanks go to Matt Witt, my multitalented son, who created the cover for this book. Even as a child, he had an eye for color and design, and it was a special pleasure to see him take my input and create something far beyond what I imagined.

DESIGNER BABIES

Volume Three

Passing the Torch

CHAPTER ONE

For the tenth time in his fifteen years, Adam Clayborn was celebrating his birthday on *Rare Air*, with Larry Knewell. Joining him were Madeline Blaze and Ensley Springer, who followed him as the second and third designer babies on the planet. Although they were the first three special children, their births unleashed a tidal wave of other parents making the same decision in the intervening years. The changes brought about by this technical revolution triggered everything from ripples of change, to tsunami-sized transformations throughout societies around the world.

Larry's show had thrived in the upheaval their births heralded, and he always welcomed their returns to his show. "Happy fifteenth, Adam, and congratulations on becoming the third richest man in the world. How does it feel to accomplish this at such a young age?"

Adam looked as if he hadn't aged a day in the past ten years, and his tailored Italian suit accented his buff build. With his gene edit for accelerated growth and development, he appeared and acted like a twenty-five-year-old adult since he was five. His low laugh before answering was natural and confident. "Money is like snow, Larry. After a few feet why bother measuring? I've been blessed with success and I'm most proud of two things. The good my microbank has done for small entrepreneurs around the globe, and the positive impact on climate change we've achieved working with Third Rock Sustainability. My personal wealth ranking doesn't matter, and besides, I've taken the pledge to donate most of my money anyway. I think it's the right thing for people like me who have been blessed with so much material success."

While these three hadn't aged, Larry had. These were to be among his final few interviews with this special trio and he spoke from the heart. "It's been a privilege to be a small part of presenting your amazing story to the world." He paused, moving from his nostalgic mood back into his role of host, aiming for ratings. "And yet, even with all your notable accomplishments, life isn't always perfect, even if your genome is."

The comment hit close to home, and Adam shot a quick glance to his left toward Ensley. While so many parts of his life thrived in the past few years, his personal life had been messy, and too many headlines in tabloids and twitter laid bare his personal failings. His words were even and measured, guessing Larry was referencing his and Ensley's very public divorce. "As your viewers know, I made mistakes that would sink any marriage, regardless of wealth. I'm just glad Ens and I worked our way back to being friends."

With the veiled reference to Adam's affairs, Larry smiled. "We'll come back to you in a moment, Adam. But first let's check in with your friends." His eyes moved to the next guest to be introduced. "Ensley, it's good to see you as well. Congratulations on being named Director of the Twenty-Three Chromosomes Foundation, the largest advocacy group for genetically modified people in the world."

Flipping back her silky black hair, she answered with determination. "Thank you, Larry. Discrimination against GM people has continued to grow in the past ten years. Things like banning scholarships at public universities, higher tax rates and quotas on civil service employment have blossomed around the planet. We didn't choose how we were born, and I find it offensive for any of us to be discriminated against through no fault of our own."

Larry's smile changed subtly with a mischievous twist at the corners. "I understand, and we'll come back to that in a moment. But first, do you agree with Adam's assessment of your relationship?"

Ensley's dark eyes narrowed, and a sadness matching her black pencil dress seemed to transmit through the camera lens. "Friends... hmm. I might have chosen the word 'civil', but yeah, we're in a somewhat better place now that our split is official and some time has passed." She looked down, took a deep breath, then exhaled slowly. Raising her head, she stared straight at Larry, her voice unsteady. "This is what I'm talking about. That WAGE group has grown in every part of the world and paints GM people as some kind of alien species, but we're very human in every way." She glanced toward Adam. "Our feelings get hurt, just like people without gene modifications."

Pleased with the start of the interviews, Larry looked left and continued the introductions. "Welcome back, Madeline. A lot is going on in your life as well. Tell us about the new tour."

With her long hair in an ombre style flowing from light to dark purple, her pure-white skin seemed almost ghostly. "The *Bumps in the Night* tour has been my biggest yet, and I haven't decided if it's in spite of the Pure Human protests or because of them." Her big smile radiated happiness. "And I don't care!"

Larry chuckled. "You seem very happy these days. Does that have something to do with the new man in your life?"

Madeline glanced off stage toward a tall, muscular guy. "Rex has been a godsend on this tour. His firm provides world class security, and we've gotten very close. He's special in so many ways."

That was the answer Larry was hoping for. "Special, yes. But as I understand, not entirely human."

Leaning back and crossing her arms, Madeline answered. "I like to say he's human plus... in all the best ways, if you know what I mean."

Blushing, Larry continued, sure the ratings meter just climbed. "I'll take your word for that, Madeline. But here's where things get, for lack of a better word, complicated. Please correct me if I get anything wrong."

"I will, don't worry."

Larry picked up reading glasses and took a quick look at his notes. "My research shows that Rex is a clone, retired from the private army, Anywhere Solutions, which is staffed entirely by hundreds of thousands of mercenary soldiers genetically identical to him. How am I doing so far?"

Her head tilted side to side. "Umm, lose the word mercenary. It's so pejorative. Otherwise, you're on the money."

Larry looked offstage toward Rex. "And he...they, all have snippets of animal DNA embedded in their genome? Things like a vertical slit pupil from a cat in their left eye to enhance night vision and a bit of dung beetle genes that increases their strength? Do I have that right?"

Madeline nodded approvingly. "Nailed it. Isn't it great? Isn't *he* great?"

Removing his glasses, Larry turned back toward Ensley. "Where does the Twenty-Three Chromosomes Foundation stand on individuals like Rex? Are you fighting for his rights as well?"

Ensley's brow wrinkled as she glanced at her friend. "It's complicated, and we haven't landed on our final position on extraspecies genetic editing. Right now, our hands are full dealing with the discrimination against people like us. Those with twenty-three purely human genes."

"It *is* very complicated." Larry continued as Ensley nodded. "And you, Adam. How do you feel about...how did Ensley phrase it? Extra-species edits."

Adam leaned toward Madeline, and the image of her in a coma three years ago after another overdose flashed, and he was glad for her recovery. "With all that my friend has been through, I'm just happy for her. I'll leave labels for other people."

With a show full of guests on this topic still to come, Larry stared into camera one to wrap up the segment. "Fifteen years ago, this was all so simple. Three cute babies came on *Rare Air* and we wondered where it would all lead. Now we're seeing some of the fallout from the decisions to modify our wiring. Society is dividing along genetic lines in both attitudes and laws. Where this will lead is still to be decided, but wherever it goes, you can be sure we'll keep you informed here on *Rare Air*."

Once off of the set, the three plus Rex stood around not knowing exactly what to say or do next. Like other young people who had once been close, the demands of their individual lives had pulled them in different directions. Interactions that had at one time been natural had lost their instinctiveness, so Adam made a suggestion. "I bought the old building where Chalky's used to be, and turned it into something new. Care to join me for dinner? I would love to catch up with everything that's going on with you guys."

Maddy reacted first by grabbing Rex's hand. "We'd love to come. The place was always so special to us and I can't wait to see what you've done with it." She glanced at Rex, almost as if asking for permission. "Right?"

The square-jawed soldier dressed in jeans and a company logoed dry-fit polo shirt stretched over a chiseled chest replied simply. "Anything you want, dear."

Adam turned to Ensley, who hadn't yet committed to the plan. He knew how badly his indiscretions had hurt her, and while he couldn't go back in time and undo the damage, he desperately hoped to get their relationship back to a better place. He spoke in all humility, hoping for a morsel of mercy. "You used the word 'civil' with Larry. I promise this won't be uncomfortable. Join us, please? For old-time's sake?"

They waited as she seemed to weigh the pros and cons. With a sigh and wave of her hand, she delivered her verdict. "I guess it's time to let go of some things." She shrugged her shoulders. "Let's go before I change my mind."

Adam felt relieved and grateful. "Thank you, Ens. I know I've still got a long way to go to get back to friends. Let this be the first step."

CHAPTER TWO

The foursome arrived in three vehicles at the location formerly housing Chalky's Wild World. Maddy and her new boyfriend traveled together, while Adam and Ensley rode separately with their own security teams, signifying the current relationship between them all. In place of the dance club was the sleek exterior of a restaurant called Memory Lane, written in neon blue script letters five feet high. Adam felt proud. "This place reminded me of all the good and bad that happened to us ten years ago, and I couldn't stand to see it sitting empty. I hope you like what I've done with it."

Entering, Maddy said what many others had before. "Wow. Something for everyone."

The smile on Adam's face widened as he pointed to a second-floor balcony area. A wave of nostalgia swept over him. "I kept the old VIP section almost the same. So many good memories up there."

Ensley noticed the section in the back. "Red tufted leather booths - dim lighting. Kind of gives that space a speak-easy vibe. Nice."

Even Rex commented. "I like the plants. They're everywhere

and I feel close to nature, even in the city."

Adam felt his cheeks warm. "I couldn't settle on a single style, so I went eclectic. Same with the menu. Let's head up to the loft, for old time's sake."

When they arrived at the owner's table, a waitress popped by to take drink orders. Ens and Maddy stared as she spoke in a rapid clip through bright green painted lips. "Mojitos are the featured drink tonight, so what's your pleasure?"

After everyone's order was taken, Maddy seemed to speak for her and Ens. "Where did you find her? She looks just like Kiss Me Kimee."

Adam's chin dipped and he spoke sheepishly. "That's her cousin. The resemblance is uncanny, isn't it?"

Ens looked pale and asked incredulously. "Why would you have her here...dressed like that? Even her miniskirt looks the same."

Determined not to be defensive, he bore his soul. "My relationship with Kimee was very complicated, and her death was tragic and senseless. A madman pulled the trigger but I've always felt more than a little responsible for what happened to everyone that night. Us hanging out here so often played a part on why he chose to shoot this place up." Just thinking of what happened on that dark night ten years ago still made his stomach churn. "I know this is going to sound weird, but during remodeling, I swore I could feel her spirit. Then one day Paige walked in, dressed like that, and I almost fell over. It was like kismet, so I hired her on the spot."

Paige returned with the drinks and winked at each person as she set their beverages on logoed coasters. "Brad will be here with menus in a few. Ciao!" With that she walked away, her hips swinging the tasseled bottom of her skirt, just like Kimee back in the day.

Ens stared at him with eyes focused like lasers. "You two

aren't..."

"No! No!" Adam's eyes were as wide as saucers. "Nothing like that, I swear." Now his startled blue eyes moistened. "But I am paying her college tuition." He put the back of his hand against his right eye, catching a single tear before it ran down his cheek. "Kimee was working so hard to get her degree it seemed the right thing to do, you know? I'm trying to balance my karma."

Brad arrived just in time to break the awkward mood as he passed out menus. "Tonight's specials are roast duck in a citrus balsamic sauce paired with mashed pumpkin, or New York's best feta pepperoni pizza. Any questions?"

Maddy shook her head. "You said eclectic. Now I get it." She opened the folded menu. "I'll need a few minutes." With that Brad nodded and headed toward the kitchen.

Adam spoke pensively. "Remember the time those thugs burst in here and cracked my skull?"

Maddy reacted. "What I recall is the revenge we plotted."

"Yeah." Ens continued the story. "We hired that security outfit to snatch Becky and Kelley off the street, and we threatened their lives." Her head slowly went side to side as she recalled the event. "Back then, I was mature in so many ways, and absolutely juvenile in so many others."

"There's no doubt we've lived crazy lives." Adam turned to Maddy. "I meant what I said to Larry, you look very happy, and that makes me feel great. From your Instagram feed, it looks like life is treating you well."

She reached for Rex's hand. "I've had more than my fair share of ups and downs since we hung out here, but these last few months have been among the best." Her gaze went to her boyfriend. "Being sober and finding someone I have so much in common with makes a huge difference." After a second, she returned the same basic question. "I hear a lot about your business success, but not much else these days. What have you been up to?"

"This place was my latest venture, and I love the way it's turned out, but frankly, I'm kind of bored and looking for my next project. I don't know what it will be, but something will turn up, I can just feel it." Adam glanced toward Ensley. "I still follow you on Twitter, and your feed has been almost nonstop. Are you working seven days a week these days?"

The blush was instant. "I preach to others about healthy living, but my work-life balance is way out of whack." She looked at them with wide eyes, seeming exasperated. "It's just that WAGE group grows stronger by the day. I worry that if I slow down, they'll make all modified people's lives even tougher."

The mention of WAGE cast a momentary pall over the table, so Adam turned to a more pleasant memory. "Remember how Yori could get the crowd dancing? He was the best." The cloud lifted, and for the next three hours there were lots of stories told over fantastic food and drinks. On a couple of occasions, the old mood of their freedom-filled-youth briefly infused the evening.

For the most part Rex had listened, smiled and once in a while laughed, though rarely spoke until midnight. "Maddy, it's time for us to go. You have a media blitz tomorrow."

She was in a rare mood. "Fuck the media. I'm hang'in with my friends tonight."

Grabbing her hand, Rex spoke low and firm. "You hired me for a reason, remember? I said it's time to go."

As if suddenly recalling a secret, Maddy's mood changed in a flash as she looked up at the powerfully built man, her words sounding timid. "Right. It's time for us to go." She stood and gave Ens a hug, before walking around the table to Adam. "I love your place. We'll have to do this again." With that, and a peck on his cheek, she put her hand in Rex's and walked away.

When they were out of earshot, Ens spoke her mind. "What the hell was that?"

Leaning back, Adam shook his head. "It was like he had some kind of mind control over her. I've *never* seen Madeline Blaze act that way."

Ens crossed her arms. "I don't like what I just saw. Something's wrong."

Adam's hand went to his chin as he weighed what he had witnessed. "Let's not jump to conclusions. She's had a lot going on with her father passing last year and her third stint in rehab. Maybe she gave him some kind of orders to keep her from slipping."

Not seeming convinced, Ens watched them walk out the door with Maddy now a step behind Rex. "I hope that's all it is."

With just the two of them remaining in the VIP area, it felt like they had the entire restaurant to themselves. Adam leaned forward speaking from the heart. "I know I've said it before, but I really am sorry I messed things up between us. One affair, maybe you could forgive... but two...in one year. I'm only surprised you tried so hard. You deserve better."

Dark eyes bore into him for long time in a stare he couldn't quite decipher. When she answered, her words were devoid of emotion, as if stating facts in a court case. "You couldn't keep it in your pants, and that's on you. But our travel schedules were insane. We *both* put the passion for our careers ahead of our marriage. I looked at my calendar after our divorce was final and realized that in the year prior, we were only together eighty-five days. That was on both of us."

Paige walked up to the table. "Anything else from the bar before I clock out, boss?"

Adam glanced at Ens, who shook her head. "We're fine, Paige. Have a good night."

"Ciao." With that, she swished away.

Ens eyed him. "You sure there's nothing going on between you two?'

Adam's light laugh signaled his understanding. "I deserve that."

Now it was Ens who laughed. "Yes, you do." Her words turned a degree warmer. "It's certainly weird that she's here, but I've thought about what you said tonight, and I kind of get it. And while things got awkward between Kimee and me at the end, I know she would approve of you helping Paige with her education."

"Thanks. That means a lot coming from you."

She stood. "It was fun getting us three together tonight, and you kept your word."

"What do you mean?"

Ens put her purse strap over her shoulder, then touched his arm. "You said it wouldn't be uncomfortable, and it wasn't." She sighed. "And I guess you were right. The night did move us one step closer to friendship."

He watched her walk away. *After everything I've done, one step at a time is better than I deserve.*

CHAPTER THREE

Bree had just finished listening to the indigenous people in the Colombian jungle talk about being illegally forced from their land when she smelled the first hint of trouble. "Is that smoke?"

The head of her personal security team, rushed forward and grabbed her elbow. "We've got to get you out of here, now!"

They had almost reached the SUV to drive out of harm's way when the first shots were heard. She demanded. "What's going on?"

Turning his head to the side, he seemed to be processing the situation, then spoke in doubt. "They wouldn't, would they?" His tone changed as another burst of gunfire echoed in the rainforest. "Son of a bitch! Those illegal miners are using fire to drive us into a massacre!"

Bree's heart-rate accelerated. "What do we do? How do we get us all to safety?"

Looking around, the security chief seemed at a loss. "We don't have enough firepower to shoot our way out." He stated the obvious. "This is bad, very bad."

Bree took charge. "Form a perimeter around everyone and get

me the SAT phone, now!" The phone was brought quickly and she was relieved when Ansen answered on the second ring.

"Hey, how's the jungle?"

Rising panic colored her desperate words. "Listen! We're under attack, and I need help now!"

"What's happening? What do you need?"

"We're trapped! A fire has been set to drive us into a massacre. I need ideas, fast!"

The sound of rapid keyboard tapping traveled from New York to Colombia as she waited, eyes darting around the perilous scene. Finally, he spoke, a tremble in his voice. "There's an Anywhere Solutions base not far from your location. Hold on while I make a call!"

The few minutes she waited seemed like an eternity as screams of terror echoed and the smoke thickened. Her mind jumped as she considered her potential rescuers. *Anywhere Solutions? We can't be relying on* **them***, can we?* Then she recalled words she hadn't thought of in years. *When the decision is between living or dying....*

The phone clicked, announcing Ansen's return to the line. "There's a fleet of helicopters spinning up now! Just hold out for a little bit until the cavalry arrives."

Tongues of flame could be seen through the smoke as she coughed. "We'll hold on as long as we can."

"Come on, now. You've been through worse. Remember the night Adam was born? You giving birth surrounded by a running gun battle?"

That memory both jarred her and made her smile as the smoke swirled around, almost gagging her as she spoke hoarsely. "I wish you were here. Like back then."

"Hang on. Help's on the way."

Breathing was getting harder as the inferno grew and the wall of hellish fire crept closer. The flames seemed to growl as they leaped toward the sky. Doubt crept in and she wanted to make sure he knew what was in her heart. "If we don't make it, I want you to know how much I love you and Adam."

"Stop that! You're going to be alright. You have to believe!"

Her words choked as much from emotion as from the toxic air she took in with each gasp. "I'll believe until my last breath." She fell to her knees, losing track of time and wheezing until she heard the sound of rotors thumping, the sound growing louder by the second. "They're here!"

The first helicopter rushed overhead and began firing down on those who were trying to kill Bree and the fleeing activists. The display of firepower was overwhelming, filling the air with thousands of rounds per minute. Moments later, two other copters landed in the opening just in front of her, three men jumping out before the crafts even touched down. They sprinted toward Bree and her protective detail and one of the three identical men spoke. "Mrs. Bree Battle?"

"Yes. That's me."

The soldier's words sounded like an order. "Come with me."

Bree pointed to the group of activists and her team. "I'm not going anywhere until you promise me you will save them all."

He grabbed her forcefully. "As we speak, the road is being cleared for a land escape. They will all be safe, but our orders are that you're leaving with us." He tugged, firmly. "Come with me, now."

She put the phone to her ear. "We're going to make it. I love you and I'll call soon." She ended the call as she was loaded into one of the choppers, then lifted off toward an unknown destination. As she took in clean air above the raging jungle fire, she shouted, trying to be heard over the noise of the rotors. "Those bastards tried to kill me and the people who have lived here for eons. Who do they think they are?"

The same soldier who had spoken on the ground, replied. "All I know is that we were sent on an extraction mission. You're safe and that's all that matters, though we did have to kill a few of them to make that happen."

His casual explanation jarred her senses, then a thought came to mind. "Where are we going?"

"We're on our way to the Anywhere Solutions South American headquarters, outside of Bogota."

With the flames fading in the distance, she took a closer look at the three soldiers riding with her. She had seen news stories on this army and these men, but it was her first time meeting them in person. They were all identical, with deep blue eyes that didn't match. One was normal, with a round pupil, while the other had a vertical slit pupil, like a cat. With a few minutes to study them closer, she saw that they were like twins, *almost* identical, but with subtle differences. She asked. "How did you get the scar?"

The muscular man smiled as he touched his cheek. "Stopping an assassination attempt on a Sheik." His smile broadened. "Those guys tip well when you save their life."

Bree made a mental note to tip him. "What's your name?"

"I'm K-Eleven-Two-Zero-Three, but my friends call me Ike."

"Oh." The fact that he answered with some kind of serial number first, instead of a real name shocked her.

She was about to ask another question when he spoke. "We're beginning our descent, so hold on tight." The drop was swift, but the touchdown was feathery smooth. When she stepped out, she was surprised to see another face she had only seen in magazines or on television, the founder and sole owner of Anywhere Solutions.

He extended his hand and spoke with a slight Russian accent. "Mrs. Battle, I'm Rolan Volkov, and I've wanted to meet you for a very long time. We have so much to discuss."

CHAPTER FOUR

Bree looked around the sprawling base as Rolan escorted her from the copter. Her words carried an air of wonder as they boarded a converted golf cart. "This place is huge... I had no idea."

"This is the largest of our six regional bases." He seemed to speak with pride. "It's bigger than Fort Campbell in the US, and I like to think my soldiers are even better trained than the Hundred and First Airborne Division based there." After a lengthy drive they approached a building marked VIP Guests. "The receptionist will show you to a suite where you can freshen up before dinner."

"Dinner? Can't I just catch a ride to Bogota, and a flight back home?"

"Of course." He smiled. "But your staff here in Colombia will remain in danger from those that mean them harm. Wouldn't you like to talk about resources we have available to protect them?"

The memory of nearly burning alive rushed back. While she had been offered assurances that everyone from the fire scene had been protected, her thoughts hadn't advanced to what comes next. She answered cautiously. "Perhaps that's a good idea."

Inside, the nondescript building resembled a luxury hotel, complete with its own brand of soap and little shampoo bottles in the extravagant bathroom. The bellman offered. "Should you want your clothes laundered, there is a robe in the closet. We can have them cleaned and back to you in under an hour." He pointed to the door. "Just hang them on the outside knob in the bag provided."

The black smoke of the jungle clung to her like a second layer of skin. "I'll think about it." Bree's mind wondered back fifteen years to the time she entered Kristoff's mansion, pregnant with Adam. *I went there afraid, then all of my expectations were turned upside down.*

After calling Ansen to let him know she was okay, and placing her khaki clothing outside the door, she eyed the oversized tub and spoke to herself. "When I woke this morning, this was not how I expected to end my day."

A long soak ensued, then she found her clothes cleaned, pressed and without even a hint of smoke, hanging outside her suite. A note accompanied them which she read aloud as she closed the door. "You are invited to dinner at seven. A car will be outside for your convenience." She studied the message. *I don't know what I expected from Anywhere Solutions, but it certainly wasn't this.*

At the appointed time she was driven to another building, that from the outside, looked like any other warehouse in the complex. When the doorman opened the door, she saw that it was far from typical.

A chandelier hung above each of the ten tables in a spacious room, with Rolan dressed in a camo uniform, rising from a chair as she entered. "Mrs. Battle, I hope you found the accommodations to your liking."

There was no need to exaggerate. "It's certainly not what I anticipated."

He motioned to an adjacent seat. "Please, join me for dinner. You must be starved after the day you've experienced."

He spoke the truth, as her stomach growled aloud, causing a shy laugh. "You timing continues to be impeccable."

As the two sat down at the table with a white linen tablecloth, he offered, "Would you like a glass of wine? Perhaps a Chilean Syrah, or Australian Chardonnay?"

Hoping for fish, she answered. "The chardonnay, if seafood is on the menu."

A wide smile met her response. "The chef prepares a wonderful sea bass, if that is to your liking."

She answered as if at a fine restaurant, instead of on a mercenary army base. "Delightful." With wine poured, and loaves of warm bread with sculpted pats of butter offered and sampled, Bree shifted the conversation. "When we first met, you said we had much to discuss. I've been wondering what you mean?"

"Yes." A small nod met her question. "The first item is simple. You run a global concern that often operates in dangerous places. I run a business that provides extraordinary levels of protection in the very same locales. I would like to make a global bid to provide Third Rock Sustainability security at any location around the globe, on a moment's notice."

Thinking of her rescue today made it easy to answer. "I would probably be dead if not for your team. That alone means that I will consider your proposal... but I know it can't be cheap. Don't forget, our foundation is a non-profit NGO. We count our pennies."

He waved his hand and his light Russian accent thickened. "Not to worry. We have special pricing levels for organizations like yours, you know, ones trying to make the world better for future generations."

For some reason his words reminded her of the secret Tree of

Life oath and a charge ran through her body. *Could it be?* Considering that she was alone on a military base in the middle of nowhere, she hoped she was wrong. "Then we would be pleased to review your bid." She took a sip of wine, then redirected the conversation. "You mentioned this was the first item. What else is on your agenda?"

A waiter appeared with their food. "With your sea bass, the chef has prepared a ginger vegetable stir fry fresh from our garden, and purple Peruvian potatoes from just across the border. I hope you enjoy."

Rolan extended his hand. "First, we enjoy a wonderful meal, then we talk business. Yes?"

The plate was a stunning display of color and the aroma made her mouth water. "Agreed."

After forty-five minutes of delicious food and small talk, Bree rounded the conversation back to business, feeling the need to uncover any secret agenda. "Thank you for a wonderful meal. Truly one of the best I've tasted in years." She wiped her mouth with the stark white napkin. "It's been a long day for me, so perhaps we talk now, before I call it a night?"

"Of course, but would you like the chef to prepare a crème brûlée for dessert? Our discussions shouldn't take long."

Her eyebrows arched and her mouth watered again. "You have excellent taste, Mr. Volkov. That would be a nice way to end the evening."

He nodded toward the waiter, then turned back to Bree. "Please, call me Rolan. We're very informal around here."

Bree couldn't stop her eyes from scanning the opulent room, but answered courteously. "Of course, Rolan."

Shifting, he seemed to settle in a comfortable position. "I see you and I as very similar. We both experienced great suffering and then turned to science to provide a path forward for the next generation of our family."

Bree had heard about what Rolan had done, but wanted to hear the story in his words. "Tell me how you see our similarities."

He folded his hands together, looking relaxed. "My son was my everything, and when he was taken from this world, I was heartbroken."

"I'm sorry for your loss. I can't imagine the pain of losing a child."

"Thank you for the kind words." He tilted his head toward her. "And as I understand, you were left sterile following your experimental brain cancer treatment."

This was the public story that she had told from the beginning, and it was true...as far as it went. She began to suspect where he was headed. "And we both turned to science for help."

A broad grin appeared. "Exactly. You with the first genetically modified child, and I with the first genetically modified clone, of my son. I view us both as pioneers of a grand new world."

"But there are differences." She felt a chill, and bumps pimpled her arms. "Adam is fully human, while your cloned...army... has genes from several other species inserted in their genome."

Rolan's gaze remained serene, not a muscle twitched. "You must understand two important things. First, these men in my army, my sons, have more than ninety-nine-point-nine percent the same genome as every other human on the planet. True, they have special traits, but so does your son. Correct?"

Bree rolled the napkin under the table, always wary of accidentally saying something that would reveal how special Adam, Ensley and Madeline really were. "I guess you could say that. We did accelerate his development. But that's not the same."

His eyes widened. "Perhaps, but a large segment of the world views them very similar, both considered abominations. That WAGE group makes the point every day."

Her jaw stiffened at the mere utterance of the group's name. "What do you propose?"

Opening his hands, he made his pitch. "You are part of an active community of GM families who do an extraordinary job of coordinating messages to the world to fight this discrimination... yet it's not enough. I have millions of dollars and leverage in governments far and wide...yet it's not enough. Both modified people and all of my men are still considered second class citizens by a significant percentage of the global population." He leaned forward, his eyes piercing. "I propose we join forces and work in coordination, for the good of all."

Silence ruled the room for a moment, until the waiter brought the dessert to the table and used a torch to caramelize the fine sugar atop the dessert. The surface hardened and turned a glistening toasted brown. With his final touch complete he left them alone. She spoke. "That's an interesting proposal. How do you see it working?"

Rolan's eyes seemed to catch the light. "We leave details for another time. Tonight is for agreeing in principle. Can we work together?"

Things had gone in a completely different direction than she anticipated, and she needed time to think. Luckily, truth was on her side. "You speak for your entire organization, while I'm part of a broad network with teams of lawyers. I'll take your proposal forward, but can't guarantee how it will be received."

"That is an excellent place to end our discussion. Please, enjoy." With that, he used his spoon to crack the shimmering sugary surface, as if breaking glass. "I'll be in the US on business next week. Perhaps we can meet then, maybe with your husband? I've admired his career from afar, and I sense the beginning of new and exciting opportunities."

The chill bumps returned upon hearing his response.

CHAPTER FIVE

A rising sun sparkled through the leaves of red maple trees at Camp Nipmuck, a place founded on the principle of helping young people deal with identity issues. Becky Brown was already in the commercial kitchen leading the team that prepared meals for the campers who arrived each week seeking adventure and a nurturing environment. Her perky, positive tone set the mood for the staff. "Breakfast line opens in ten minutes."

When the doors opened a steady stream of youths, aged eleven through seventeen, carried their trays from station to station, filling their plates with fluffy eggs and syrup drenched pancakes. She watched with pride over the buzzing chunky wooden tables filled with smiling kids enjoying a week away from daily challenges back home. As often happened, she was deep in thought when Kelley arrived with their ten-year-old son, nicknamed Benz. It was the combination of his given first and middle names, Benjamin Ezra. *I wish something like this had been around when I was their age.*

Snapping out of her mental drift, she spied them getting their meal. Joining them, she rubbed her son's head. "Ready for a day on the lake?"

His gap-toothed smile warmed her. "You bet, mom."

As he attacked his breakfast with gusto, Kelley reached for Becky's hand. "The kitchen's running like a well-oiled machine.

You make it look easy."

"I keep operations running smoothly while you handle accounting and dealing with demanding parents. I clearly have the easier job!"

Now it was Kelley who sounded contemplative. "Remember how hard it was in the beginning? We left WAGE with a few thousand dollars and a hope and prayer of making a new life."

"I was scared." Becky kept her voice low. "Scared of the Society exposing our secret, and what WAGE would do to us if they found out."

Looking around at the spotlessly clean dining room, Kelley mused. "Remember what this place was like when we found it? There wasn't a single building that was fit for humans."

"I'm proud that we did most of the repairs and remodeling ourselves. Every nail driven and weed pulled brought us one step closer to our dream." Becky's eyes moistened. "And pounding those nails and ripping out those thistles gave me time to start on the road toward getting my head right. Watching Benz grow up helped me see how wrong I was about genetic modification. The answer was right there in front of me, and it took my life almost falling apart to see it. Inclusion is the answer, not exclusion. I wouldn't have made it without you by my side. You're my rock."

Kelley squeezed her hand at the compliment, then her tone turned serious. "Right now, I'm worried about next week. We've got one very demanding grandmother bringing her granddaughter here."

Becky's spine stiffened at the mention of Lesedi Khomalo, the woman who took over as Chairwoman of WAGE upon their exit. She whispered. "We've kept Benz's secret for ten years, surely we can for one more week. If not, she will make it her mission to destroy everything we've worked for."

The easy smile on Kelley's face tightened. "We've stayed distant but cordial all these years, and now we have something new in common. With her granddaughter identifying as gay, we can keep her distracted by focusing on all we're doing to make her life easier than we had."

The years of therapy helped Becky tamp down her rising rage. She simply laid out what was at stake. "But if she were to find out, our taxes would be raised as parents of a GM child, putting our business at risk. Then there's 'The List.'"

Kelley's eyes darted at Benz as if drawn magnetically. "It's not law here yet, as in many places, but WAGE updates the national database of known GM children on their own every day. Lesedi would trumpet his name if she ever finds out. Thank God Chavez and the Society kept their word."

"Chavez. Another name that turns my mouth sour."

Moving her hand to Becky's shoulder, they both looked at the happy boy. "I know you hate how it all went down, but look at what she gave us. He's so smart, and we both see our father's resemblances... but without those hot tempers. I would do it all again, wouldn't you?"

Becky felt her cheeks warming. "You two are the best things that have ever happened to me. I never dreamed how deeply I could love him."

Rubbing her wife's shoulder, Kelley's words sounded optimistic. "One week, a few interactions, that's all. Trust me, nothing's going to go wrong."

CHAPTER SIX

After her time in New York on business and getting re-acquainted with her friends, Maddy and Rex flew to the west coast to wrap up the final loose ends of her father's estate. He had been dead nearly a year, but the complicated financial ties had taken forever to untangle. Standing in front of the fireplace of her parent's former home, she was lost in memories, staring at the Nobel Prize Ray had received posthumously. *If only he and Dr. Chavez had discovered the cure to Huntington's Disease a few months earlier.*

Rex walked up behind her and wrapped her in his arms. "I wish I had met him. Sounds like he was a great man."

"He was a brilliant scientist." She half-laughed. "And he knew how to both put up with my mother *and* make her happy. That might have been his most impressive skill."

Reflecting on how her life could have been different if he had survived, a melancholy mood engulfed her. Turning, she headed to the deck overlooking the pacific. "I need some fresh air to clear my head."

Once outside, she stood next to the rail, soon joined by Rex, her white crochet bikini cover fluttering in the breeze. Thinking about her father had led her to wonder about how Rex felt about his biological background. "You know my story, so how about you? I know what I've read, but we've never really talked about it."

Her question about his unusual genetic background didn't seem to faze him at all. "It's pretty cut and dry. I was born clone K-Twelve-Eight-Zero-Six, and went to work for Anywhere Solutions as soon as I was legally allowed. I'm one of the few who has stepped away, and now I'm Rex DeMan, owner of Rex Solutions, a small private security company for the rich and famous."

"Come on." Sensing he was in a good mood, she poked his ribs. "That's about the most abridged biography I've ever heard. What about your mother, your childhood...your relationship with your father?"

She felt his body tense. "Father." Several seconds passed with only the sound of the waves below. "We never use that word."

"Oh." Maddy was now unsure about Rex's mood, but she had to know more if this relationship had any chance of developing beyond a fling with a bodyguard. And she *so* wanted that. She had been alone, trying her best to stay clean but feeling on edge about slipping when she met him. It was one of her lowest points, and he had swept her off her feet with grand romantic gestures when she needed them most. Now things were moving fast. "How about your mother? Your brothers?"

He stepped back, his face contorted, and he slapped her hard, sending her stumbling backwards a few steps before tripping and landing on her backside. He was by her side in an instant, full of apologies. "Oh, Maddy! I'm so sorry. I don't know what came over me. I'll never do anything like that again, I swear!"

She rubbed her cheek as tears sprang, simultaneously stunned, angry and frightened. Her words lacked bravado or swagger. "What the hell, Rex? Son of a bitch, that hurt."

"I promise on my very life. I'll never do anything like that again." He sounded frantic. "I'll make it up to you. Maybe dinner at Nobu?"

She inched back, still on the ground, wanting to put some space between them. "You better never do anything like that again."

The large man groveled. "Please forgive me. I'll tell you anything you want to know." As she started to stand, he jumped to his feet, then pulled her up as easily as picking up a quarter from the pavement. "I mean it. Ask me anything you want." He went back down on both knees and looked up, pleading. "Please, please forgive me. It will never happen again."

Staring down at him, her mind splintered and she didn't know what to say, so she bought some time. "Stay here, I need a minute." She headed straight for the bathroom to check the mirror for signs of bruising, talking to her reflection. "Just some redness, the bastard better be thankful for that."

As she gazed, her mind went to his last words, asking for forgiveness and promising it would be the last time anything like this happened. Her thoughts bounced. *You said that when you yelled at me last week. What the hell have you been through? Can I ever trust you?* Staying in the house for nearly an hour, she regained her composure, trying to figure out what she wanted to do. *I have to know more, and he better tell me the truth, or we're finished.*

When she returned, she found him in the exact same position as she had left him, on his knees. He looked up at her like a dog who knew they had done something wrong and begged for forgiveness through their eyes. She demanded. "Tell me something real, something that most people don't know about you and the others."

She could almost see the wheels turning as he decided what to share. "Okay, let's see." He wiped his mouth. "Everyone knows how alike we look, and that we're genetically identical, leading most to make the assumption that we're almost the same. As strange as it may sound, the truth is nearly the complete opposite."

Maddy's head snapped, as she thought he might be lying.

"Really? You're going to have to explain that."

Still on his knees, he leaned back, lowering onto his heels, his muscular shoulders slumping. "We're all genetically the same, but we're carried by surrogates in locales around the world. The women who carry us are mostly poor and desperate, that's how Rolan keeps costs down. I was born in the Philippines, while the serial number following me was born in Bulgaria. We mature fast, like you and your two friends, but we spend our first three years being cared for by those women in their homes. All of us have completely different childhood experiences."

"Wow. I didn't know that." Maddy's curiosity was piqued. "What was your home like?"

"Maria, I was never allowed to call her mother, was a decent woman. With the money Rolan sent, she made sure I had everything on his demanding list. As you might imagine, that didn't always sit well with her biological children who made do with less, or with her husband, Oscar. He despised me, but Rolan made it clear that physical abuse would have swift and harsh consequences, though Oscar stepped over that line, hitting both me and Maria frequently. Only when I joined his army did I learn that some had it better, and some had it far worse. It's the old nature versus nurture debate, except this is being done on a massive scale with genetics as the only constant in a sea of variables."

God. I had no idea about any of this. No wonder he's so fucked up. Her mind raced, needing to know more. Her word flowed fast. "And once you joined this private army? What was that like?"

His head shook and she could see him travel back in his mind to his youth, his protective façade melting in front of her. "In the beginning, it was the best and worst thing that had ever happened. Remember, we were all three-years old, but equivalent in intelligence, size and strength to sixteen-year-olds, all with identical genomes. The drill sergeants were the same as us, except older and stronger. If a two-mile run seemed too hard, you couldn't make any excuses, because the cadet next to you was doing it, and you had identical genes. They pushed us hard because they knew exactly how much we could withstand."

His revelations blew her away, painting a childhood so foreign and different from her own upbringing. "So, you're all different, but also the same."

"You just summed up the Anywhere Solutions army. The soldiers feel a bond with each other, like no other fighting force in the world, and would do anything to protect one another. That camaraderie was the best thing about serving together, and the single reason most never leave."

Maddy looked down at Rex, her anger beginning to soften as she learned the source of his rage. "But you left. Why?"

She could see the muscles in his jaw ripple before he unclenched and replied. "We were never allowed to call him father, only General Volkov, or Boss. But genetically speaking, that's what he is. For most, it's no big deal, but for some reason a few of us see it different. I can't really explain it, but from the first time I met him, I was determined to do something that would make him notice *me*, as an individual. It quickly became apparent that wouldn't happen in a sea of men doing the same jobs with almost identical intelligence and physical skill."

"Kind of like a kid wanting to stand out in a big family."

He nodded. "Except we're all twins, and number in the tens of thousands. I knew if I was going to have any chance of catching his attention, I would have to do it on the outside. So, I saved my paychecks and when I had enough, I set out on my own. Like I said, that made me an exception, as most of my brothers chose to never leave. I looked around, and this business was the best match for my skill set, so here I am. What I didn't expect was to meet someone like you, someone who connected with me as an individual, someone who liked me for who I was from the day we met."

Those words touched her heart. "You *are* someone special, and there's no one else in the world exactly like you."

His eyes glistened. "I may not deserve it, but I'm begging. Please forgive me."

She reached toward him, offering to pull him up, understanding what drove him like never before...but still wary. "I will forgive you this time, but it better not happen again...ever. And a *week* of dinners at Nobu sounds delightful."

CHAPTER SEVEN

Larry had landed the only interview that Rolan Volkov would be doing on this trip to the States, and he was ready. He primed his audience as Rolan sat on the adjoining sofa. "In the past fifteen years, our world has been irrevocably changed with genetically modified humans now numbering in the millions. Our next guest is proving that genetic modification may only be the beginning. He has cloned his deceased son, and added edits that include splicing in genes from different species. Not only has he taken this step to enhance certain traits, but he has repeated the process tens of thousands of times, creating a literal army of super soldiers. We have a lot to cover, so let's welcome Rolan Volkov, CEO of Anywhere Solutions, the largest private army in the world."

Rolan seemed relaxed, wearing fatigues and black boots, looking like the soldier he was. "Thank you, Larry. It's my pleasure to share my story with your audience."

Reveling in this scoop, Larry began. "Take us back to the beginning. Give us a glimpse of the life of young Rolan Volkov."

Rubbing salt and pepper stubble, Rolan reminisced with a grin. "I was born into privilege, but didn't fit in. I liked hanging out with tough crowds and got into a lot of trouble. One too many bar fights landed me in front of a judge who gave me two options. Join the army or go to jail." He chuckled. "That directionless young man couldn't have comprehended that decision would lead to me sitting here with you. It's been a remarkable journey."

Glancing at his notes, Larry concurred. "Your rise through the ranks to join the GRU Spetsnaz special forces was remarkable. One of the youngest ever, if my research is correct."

"I finally found an outlet for my energy and talent! If only everyone could be so lucky."

Larry leaned forward. "And as a young father, you were blessed with a son who seemed to be a chip off the block. It's not every elite soldier who gets to serve with their child. What was that like?"

The smile faded, and the exuberance of moments ago was replaced with a melancholy tone. "What started as a dream come true, quickly turned into a nightmare. My son was killed on a night mission at a location I can't disclose."

"I'm sorry for your loss. Having a child die must be one of the most difficult things in life." Having expressed sufficient sympathy, Larry pressed. "And that's when you decided to create an army of super soldiers?"

"Slow down a bit." Rolan put a hand up. "It was a very difficult time for my wife and I, and for a long time we simply shared our grief." He took in a deep breath. "But after a while, my sorrow triggered an idea. We had banked Kaiden's cord blood at birth, so had access his stem cells, giving us what we needed to create an exact copy of our son."

Larry prodded. "But you didn't stop there. Why the edits splicing other species DNA into his genome?"

Rolan's hand made a pass over his short military cut hair. "When

I found out the details of his death, I learned that it was a night mission where an enemy combatant went unseen. That started the cascade of events that culminated in his death. I began thinking, if I'm going to recreate my son, why not enhance his abilities to perhaps prevent anything like that from ever happening again?"

"That's a bridge too far for almost everyone." Larry shook his head. "You've created a new species, then made thousands of identical copies!"

A tilt of the head signaled Rolan's reply. "Not really. My sons, and that's what I call them all, still have twenty-three chromosomes and are ninety-nine-point-nine percent the same as everyone else. In fact, a few have successfully produced children with women from around the globe without the help of invitro."

A quick glance at his notes fueled Larry. "But still, they have cat DNA added for eyesight, dung beetle DNA for strength, and I'm told even a bit of border collie DNA for enhanced trainability. They are *not* completely human, no matter what you say!"

Leaning back, Rolan crossed his arms. "On that we must disagree, but one thing is indisputable. Governments and private companies around the world love them. I have a meeting at the Pentagon tomorrow to discuss expanding our contract."

Larry raised an eyebrow. "I understand why, but based on my conversations with normal Americans, many find that distasteful, to say the least."

With a sneak of a smile reappearing, Rolan uncrossed his arms. "When protesters in the street demand, 'Bring Our Troops Home,' politicians look for ways to stay in office while protecting this country's interests. They bring your sons and daughters home and fill the void with our soldiers. We handle your business for you at less cost, and no risk of American loss of life. Your citizens should count us as heroes."

With a furrowed brow, Larry conceded a bit. "I had a grandson stationed in the Mid-East last year and was glad he was shipped home before that big dust-up."

"Exactly. We fought for America's interests while your grandson was safely stateside."

Larry had one more objection. "But you would just as readily fight for America's enemies, if the price was right. Correct?"

Rolan extended his hands. "What can I say? We would never fight on different sides in the same conflict, but this is a business, the business of war. Anywhere Solutions wasn't always the biggest private army in the world, but we are now because we're the best at what we do, and the demand for our services has never been higher."

Larry now looked directly into camera one. "When genetic editing of humans became a reality, many worried about these very kinds of developments. Some downplayed the risks while other trumpeted them. We are just as polarized today with many calling these soldiers monsters, while others gladly spend millions for their services. Where it will end, I certainly don't know, but you can be certain that we'll keep you informed here on *Rare Air*."

CHAPTER EIGHT

Adam sat alone at the owner's table waiting for the group to arrive. He sought conformation as Paige strolled up. "Everything set for tonight? It's my parents first visit and I want dinner to go smoothly."

She winked, her lash extensions exaggerating the gesture. "Everyone's ready, boss." Her gaze lingered. "You okay?"

"Yeah." His words lacked conviction through his easy smile. "Just a little bored."

She looked incredulous as she pointed to one of his security team members. "Bored? How can that be? If you want to do something exciting, just snap your fingers and one of those guys will make the arrangements for anything you want."

"Look, I'm not complaining…not really, anyway. My problems are ultra-first-world issues. I've done about everything I've ever wanted. I've summitted Everest and traveled to the Mariana Trench in a sub, the deepest point on earth. I'm ready for something new."

"You rich people." She shook her head.

He shrugged. "What can I say? I guess money can't buy everything." Looking past her, he saw his eclectic collection of guests arriving, all at the same time, and being brought to the private area. "Now, *this* should be interesting. My parents, my ex and the notorious General Rolan Volkov."

"I'll go alert the kitchen, then be back for drink orders."

Out of habit he watched her walk away, reminding him again of the loss of Kimee and their unborn child. A flash of what the child she was carrying might have become, raced through his mind. *Becoming a father just wasn't meant to be.* He stood, embracing his mother a little more tightly than usual as they arrived. "It's been too long, it's so good to see you."

"You could stop by every now and then, you know." Her tease was familiar. "I assume you remember where we live."

His cheeks felt warm, knowing that she was right. A good son really should visit his mother more than he had in the past couple of years. "Yes mom, I know how to get to your place." His arms now reached for his father. "Good to see you too, dad."

Ensley extended her hand. "Dining here twice in two weeks. That's almost a habit."

The handshake felt awkward, but he was glad to see her again. "There will always be a table here for you." He caught a glimpse of his mother staring at Ensley, knowing she loved her like a daughter, and had been heartbroken by their split. "And I'm sure you're always welcome at mom and dad's place anytime as well."

"Yes! Anytime, Ens." Bree then embraced Ensley, just as she had Adam.

For the first time in a long time, he saw Ensley smile sincerely, wrapped in his mother's arms. Seeing both women happy warmed him as he turned to the formal introduction with Rolan Volkov. "Welcome to Memory Lane, General Volkov."

The general's eyes panned the restaurant. "Incredible. One can see your vision stamped on every square inch."

"Thank you." The compliment made a good impression on Adam. "Building it has been a labor of love."

After all were seated, Paige took drink orders as Brad brought warm loaves of bread served on heated stones. When everyone had a suitable beverage, Adam proposed a toast. "To good friends, family, and potential business partners."

As soon as everyone finished the first sip, Rolan raised his chilled vodka and proposed a similar toast in his native Russian language. "Za nashu druzjbu. To our friendship."

All took their second swallow, as Brad returned for their food orders. When he headed for the kitchen, Bree turned toward Rolan to make an announcement. "Rolan, I have good news. The board of Third Rock Sustainability reviewed your proposal on a global security agreement and were impressed. We'll be saving over twenty-five percent with your bid, and from what I witnessed firsthand, it will be an upgrade in quality as well."

Rolan raised his glass again, and all followed. "Vyp'yem za uspekh nashego dela! Let us drink to the success of our business!"

All joined in yet another drink, then Bree spoke again. "When we first met last week, you mentioned the idea of partnering on messaging with the GM community. I invited Ensley to join us tonight, as she is the director of the Twenty-Three Chromosomes Foundation. She is in a much better position to talk about that aspect."

Rolan seemed intent on getting everyone drunk as he once again raised a glass. "Za nashikh milikh dam. To our ladies."

Adam eyed Ens, seeing her taking the tiniest of sips at this point. *Smart. I think this guy is trying to get us sloshed. Something's off.*

"General Volkov..." Ensley began before he interrupted.

"Please, we are friends now. Call me Rolan."

"Alright, Rolan it is. While your offer is intriguing, our organization has not yet reached consensus on a stance regarding your... sons. Is that the right term to use for your soldiers?"

His nod was exaggerated. "Yes. That is the term that I prefer, and just to be clear, they all have twenty-three chromosomes, just like everyone at this table."

"I get that, Rolan." Ens took in a sharp breath as her head tilted. "It's the other changes you made that give us pause. As modified people, we live and work alongside the unmodified population, and they get to know us as individuals. Most of your sons serve in your army, making it so much easier for people to form prejudices against 'the other.' Tying us together may help in many ways, but will surely alienate in just as many, perhaps more."

Adam watched the general consider her point, his face never giving a clue as to his thinking. *He's good.*

"Then we need for you to get to know my boys. We run a leadership academy for high level executives focused on the competency of team building. We've had leaders from over fifty Fortune One-Hundred companies go through a bootcamp like experience with a platoon of new soldiers. It's a physically demanding two weeks, but the feedback we get is phenomenal. A new class starts Monday. Would you like to try it?"

Her head was shaking as Adam jumped in. "I've been searching for something out of the ordinary, and that sounds fascinating. Tell us more."

Leaning forward, the general's accent became more pronounced. "If you're looking for adventure with more than a hint of real danger, then this is for you. In addition to weapons training, there will be instruction in skydiving, night missions, and water operations, all with a focus of working as a team to improve the odds of success. It's physically demanding and a real adrenaline rush... but I must warn that these are live drills, and sometimes people do get hurt."

Adam could feel both his excitement rise as well as his parent's stares. "That sounds exactly like what I've been wanting, and you say it starts Monday?"

Clapping his hands once, Rolan answered. "You will join us, yes?"

Glancing for a second toward his mother, Adam saw a look he interpreted as sheer terror, and he hated to make her feel that way, but he didn't hesitate. "Count me in. I'll see you Monday."

Brad led a parade of servers who now surrounded the table, placing the main courses. "Enjoy. If you need anything, please let me know." With that he took his station a few feet away.

Another toast was offered, this time from Adam. "To new adventures!"

Compliments about the meals were freely offered by all for the next forty minutes. Copious amounts of alcohol lowered protective walls, giving freedom to friendly banter. By the time the plates were cleared the mood had become much more welcoming, even with Rolan. That all changed as Ansen reached for his glass of water and the general spied a glimpse of his Tree of Life tattoo peaking from his shirt cuff. "I see you have ink. My father had a remarkably similar tree etched on his wrist as well."

For a second or two, the table went completely silent until Ansen answered calmly. "I get that a lot. I just liked the design, but I hear it was a fad back in the day."

Rolan smiled like a man who had found a forgotten twenty-dollar bill in his pocket. The table talk resumed as he replied. "Yes. I'm sure that's it."

Adam's mind spun as Brad came forward, lighting individual flaming lava cakes to finish their meal. Blue flames engulfed miniature balls of chocolate, creating a festive sight. *That was weird. Good job, dad.* He changed the subject as the fire danced, not wanting to wade into a conversation so delicate with that much alcohol in his system. "Who doesn't like a little show with their dessert?"

There was no more discussion of the tattoo and the mood shifted almost back to the casual level of earlier as Rolan stood, glass in hand. "I have a meeting in Riyadh in the morning, and I've kept my plane waiting as long as I can." He raised his goblet. "Spasibo nashemu khozyainu i vsemu, chto my sobirayemsya uznat' drug o druge. Thanks to our host, and all that we are about to learn about each other." After finishing his drink, he went around the table shaking each person's hand. "Thank you for a lovely evening."

With that, he was gone, leaving the four alone at the table. Adam seemed to speak for all. "Where did that tattoo remark come from?"

The creases on Ansen's brow telegraphed his mood. "That wasn't a casual observation. I've got some research to do, and we need to have a council meeting. Soon. I don't have a good feeling about this."

Bree and Ansen made their exit next, after hugging both Adam and Ensley. She reminded him. "Don't forget where we live."

Adam chuckled. "I'll stop by, mom. I promise."

Now it was only Ensley and Adam alone at the table. She touched his arm. "You didn't have to volunteer to do that team-building thing. I'm fine if we never link up with them."

Crossing his arms as they stood watching his parents leave, his thoughts turned over possibilities as if looking for clues under rocks. "I really had been looking for a new adventure, but with that remark about dad's tattoo?" His mind raced. "Something's up with the general and I can't think of anywhere more important for me to be."

CHAPTER NINE

Becky Brown glanced out the window of their expansive log home set on the grounds of Camp Nipmuck. "When are they going to get here?"

Crossing her legs as she sat on the floral sofa while reading a magazine, Kelley gave advice. "Just chill. They'll be here when they get here."

While years of therapy had lowered Becky's anger level, it had done nothing for her impatient streak. "I just want to get this part over with. We have too much on the line." Finishing the sentence, she spied what she had been searching for, and her anxiety level spiked. "They're here."

Four large men in matching dark suits piled out of the black SUV's, opening the doors for the women they protected. Lesedi Khomalo exited first, followed by her adult daughter, Elna Mokoena. Last out was her thirteen-year-old daughter, Precious. The three generations of women made the short trek from the camp parking lot to the private home of the owners. Kelley reassured Becky. "Take a deep breath. Everything's going to be fine."

Becky waited as her nerves frayed, finally hearing the ding-dong of the doorbell. Benz bolted down the stairs, skipping three steps at a time, reaching the front door first. Pulling the door open, he greeted the visitors. "Hi!" He locked eyes with Precious. "Are you ready to have fun?"

All of the adults giggled at his excitement as the group entered the foyer. Becky arrived and reached for Lesedi's hand, conflicted in her emotions. She was seeing someone with whom she had once been close, but who now represented real danger. "It's so good to see you."

Stepping forward, Lesedi, dressed in a suit jacket with African print trimming on the lapel and sleeves, gave her a customary peck on the lips. "My old friend! It has been far too long!"

Introductions were made, then Kelley led the way into the den. "Benz, how about giving Precious a tour of the camp?"

Precious' eyes widened. "Bye mom!"

Elna waved as the two young people sped out the door. "She's been looking forward to this for a long time. It's been a rough year."

Fire and heat were never far from Lesedi's surface. "I am proud that South Africa has some of the most progressive laws regarding homosexuality on the continent, but in so many parts of the country, attitudes remain very fixed."

Becky reached for her former friend's hand, choosing her words carefully. "It's the same here. Better than in the past, but many roadblocks remain before we can all feel equal." She gestured toward the couch. "Please, make yourself at home."

When everyone settled, Elna seemed uneasy. "Precious was bullied at school this past year, and we sought counseling. It's helped, but I worry about her all the time."

"This will be a great week for her." Kelley put a comforting arm around Elna's shoulder. "Every kid here has faced the same kinds of discrimination, and understands what she's been through.

Becky and I experienced the same thing, and that's why we built this camp for these kids. We want them to have it easier than we did. I bet she makes some lifelong friends."

Seeming reassured, Lesedi turned the conversation. "Speaking of discrimination, WAGE has had some important wins recently."

"Yeah, we follow what you're doing very closely." Becky spoke the truth, but not at all like Lesedi was sure to have heard. "There are more laws in more countries than ever."

Sitting taller, the regal woman launched into recital of what seemed her favorites. "Fifty countries, including India, China and Canada have national lists published of all GM people, which has greatly reduced the number of families choosing that route. It's been a winding path, but momentum is on our side."

In her mind, Becky responded as Lesedi took a breath, but her mouth stayed closed. *Or have simply gone underground, living in fear that their secret will come out and ruin their lives. This must have been similar to how Jews felt as the Nazis came to power.*

Lesedi continued calling out new discriminations. "And I just love what's happening here in the United States. Not only are modified people ineligible for public university scholarships, but the incomes of those kinds of people are taxed higher." She laughed. "Greedy politicians are always looking for new ways to increase revenue without pissing off the masses."

Becky kept her plastic smile in place as she again spoke plainly, with one meaning for Lesedi and another for Kelley. "You've done so much."

Seeming pleased, Lesedi aimed a compliment toward her hosts. "We could never have had this success without the groundwork that you two established. It's still hard for me to fathom how you could just walk away from the cause."

Kelley fielded this one, and Becky was grateful. "You know how stressful it is running a large organization like WAGE. When Benz was born, we took inventory of our life, and realized we needed to make a change, a major change. While we've switched tracks, we remain committed to making the world a better place."

Elna spoke, relief now in her voice. "And now our paths cross again. I'm so pleased that Precious has this opportunity to experience at least a taste of what the world could be like if everyone just accepted her for who she is."

Becky's fake smile turned sincere. "Precious will be in good hands and she'll have a wonderful week."

The two youths burst back into the house. "Mom!" Words flowed excitedly from the teen. "They have a lake, and canoes, and horses. It's amazing!"

Smiling, Elna embraced her daughter. "You look so happy, I guess that means you want to stay?"

"Yes, yes! And Benz says I haven't seen half the place."

Lesedi joined her daughter and granddaughter in standing. "Then I guess it's time for us to leave so you can experience every moment of fun." She turned to Becky and Kelley. "Elna and I have business in the States, so we're only a phone call away, should any emergency arise."

Elna's worry seemed to return. "Please, take care of my only child, she's so special to us. You can tell by her name how much we love her."

Becky hugged both women, fully understanding how much a child could mean to a mother. "Every child is special and we'll watch over Precious as if she were our own. You have my word."

CHAPTER TEN

Ansen wasted no time kicking off the rare Sunday virtual council meeting. He glanced at the faces on his screen beaming in from around the globe. "I had an interesting first meeting with General Rolan Volkov of Anywhere Solutions." The mere mention of the infamous name stirred mumbling. "And after doing some research, interesting has turned to concerning."

Ensley, now a council member following the retirement of Sameer two years ago, spoke. "I was there as well, and I can assure everyone that something's off. He pitched the idea of teaming with the GM movement to normalize his soldiers to the rest of the world, then he made what I considered a veiled reference to the Society."

More grumbles echoed back to Ansen. "That's right. He made the comment when he caught a glimpse of my tattoo." Rolling up his Brooks Brothers shirt's long sleeve, Ansen displayed the inking that two other members of the council also shared. "He said his father had a similar drawing on his wrist."

Master Fong weighed in. "Interesting indeed. The Tree of Life Society had a tumultuous existence in Russia after the Bolsheviks took power in 1917."

Nodding, Ansen confirmed. "That's right, but with the fall of the Soviet Union, we began reaching out, seeking restoration of our ancient bonds. That's when we discovered the full story of what had happened in those lost seventy-plus years. It turns out that behind the iron curtain a virulent strain of eugenics had become the dominant ideology of our former members. Even today, very few from those times have returned to fellowship."

Zadie entered the conversation. "Speaking from experience, the doctrine of purity has a very strong appeal and can spread as fast and destructively as a forest fire. What has your investigation uncovered?"

"It seems that Ivan Volkov, Rolan's father, was indeed a Tree of Life member."

Dr. Chavez was blunt. "And did the apple fall far from the tree? Is Rolan a member of that ugly branch?"

Ansen shook his head. "It doesn't appear that he is. From what I've gathered, Ivan Volkov was a strict, bordering on abusive parent. Rolan grew up rebelling against everything for which his father stood. It fits with his biography of always being in trouble, then finding a home in the Russian armed forces, where he could exert power over others himself. After his father's mysterious death, he took his inheritance and has parlayed it into building his army."

Gunnar Haraldsson, the tall Swede in his second year on the council, provided perspective. "As a psychologist, I will add that it also fits with the creation of that cloned force. He seeks absolute power, so as never to be powerless again, like he was as an abused child."

As usual, Chavez cut to the chase. "What does he want? What's his game with that clone army?"

"Right now, we don't know." Ansen paused as he looked at his son in one of the squares on his screen, feeling both pride and concern. "Fortunately, we have an opportunity to insert a spy into his organization. Rolan has invited Adam to be a participant in an executive leadership training as an imbed with his soldiers."

All twelve members nodded approval as Adam addressed them. "I'm flying out this evening for what I'm told will be an intense experience. I'll learn everything I can and report back as soon as possible."

Even knowing Adam's enhanced healing abilities, Ansen's parental thoughts became words. "Just come back in one piece."

Adam's easy smile was never far from the surface. "Don't worry so much. I've learned better than to go looking for trouble."

The memory of the day that Liza Howard shot him returned unbidden as Ansen replied. "That doesn't mean it won't come looking for you. Watch your back out there."

CHAPTER ELEVEN

Adam stood at attention in a line with ten nearly identical Anywhere Solutions soldiers as part of Alpha squad. All were dressed in camouflage pattern uniforms, already blending in with the jungle behind them as the sun rose. In this remote location, surrounded by identical clones, it felt like a scene from some apocalyptic film. Adam's mind wondered. *What the hell have I gotten myself into?*

General Volkov's loud voice jolted him back mid-sentence. "... be tested like never before, but with dedication and teamwork, you'll become part of a fighting force the likes of which the world has never seen. I'll see you again in three days." Holding up two fingers in a victory sign, he yelled. "Victory is ours!"

All the troops held their hands up in the same sign, so Adam did as well, joining them in the call response. "Victory is ours!" He smothered a smile. *And so, the indoctrination begins.*

Alpha squad's leader, K-Eleven-Seven Thousand, shouted. "Backpacks on! Our five-mile warm-up begins now!"

K-Eleven, as he instructed the squad to call him, set a grueling pace through the Colombian jungle, and soon they reached a small clearing. "Full halt! Backpacks off, hydration in!"

Adam was pleased that he had kept up with his species-augmented companions. Sweat was dripping from him and everyone else in the smothering jungle heat as he whispered to the soldier that had ran in front of him on the narrow paths. "I'm glad we're easing into the training."

Catching the humor, water came out of the young man's nose as he laughed while drinking from his canteen. "Come on, man." He coughed, then laughed again. "I'm K-Fifteen-One Zero-One, but my friends call me 'Z'."

Seeing a sense of humor relaxed him. "I'm Adam. I hope we become friends, Z."

Small talk was over as K-Eleven called them together. "Your first assignment is to prepare as a team for a hand-to-hand competition. In thirty-minutes another squad will enter this clearing and a contest will begin." He stood on a dirt line that marked the diameter of the circular space, then pointed to a line halfway to the edge behind them, then another line halfway to the other end. "The first team to push, drag or otherwise move every member of the opposing team behind the opponent's quarter line is the winner."

Raising a hand, Adam called out. "And what's in it for the winners?"

K-Eleven smiled. "In addition to bragging rights, you'll feast on a lunch of burgers, pizza and beer."

That got the team talking as Adam asked the next logical question. "And the losers?"

"Bread and water...plus you carry yours and the other team's backpacks five miles farther to tonight's camp."

With the stakes set, there was only one more question for Adam to ask. "And the rules?"

Waving his right hand, K-Eleven replied. "You may use any tool the jungle provides. Nothing from your packs or anything else from the outside world allowed. Understood?" He paused, a mile-wide grin appearing on his face. "And by the way, the opposing team are special ops trainees."

A couple of random curse words came from the squad as Adam replied. "We'll figure it out."

"Then you would be the first ever to win this challenge, grunts." K-Eleven laughed derisively. "You have thirty minutes to get ready for your ass whipping."

K-Eleven walked away leaving the first day recruits alone in the middle of the forest opening. Z spoke for the other nine as all looked at Adam. "You got a plan, boss?"

Nine pairs of mismatched eyes stared at him expectantly. *This is the first time in my life I've ever felt like the oldest in a group. Feels weird.* "My overall plan is that win or lose, we do it together. Agreed?"

Yeses with different accents answered. "Alright then. Let's take an inventory of skills and experiences. Where are you guys from...what did you grow up doing?"

One by one they replied and a couple of ideas began percolating, spurred by Z's upbringing on an Argentine ranch, and K-Fifteen-Two-Two-Two, informally known as 'Duce' raised in Africa. Adam summarized what they had discovered in just a few minutes of getting to know each other. "Z has used a weapon called a bola to bring down calves, and Duce grew up on a broad savanna and knows how to take plant fiber and make cordage. Z, tell us again how these bola's work."

Z verbally sketched out the concept. "It's two weighted objects connected by a meter or so of rope. You hold one end, spin it over your head, and aim at the legs of your target as you throw it."

Adam looked at Duce. "Can you make ten cords like that in twenty minutes?"

"I'll need a lot of help, but I think so."

"Good, take five guys with you, and get started. I'll work with the others to find some chunks of deadwood to use on the ends. We'll not go down without a fight."

Adam couldn't help but notice how the soldier's movements mimicked each other, right down to the way they analyzed a piece of wood, flicking away those they deemed unsatisfactory. Then, when Z found a suitable makeshift end, he held it aloft and yelled. The others gave a thumbs up at exactly the same time. *This is going to take some getting used to.*

Twenty minutes later they had ten rudimentary weapons ready to go as Z gave a demonstration, swinging the handmade armament overhead, then launching it toward a sapling. The centrifugal force wrapped the cordage tightly around the base. "That's how it's supposed to work."

Adam's eyes widened. "I'm so impressed with what everyone has done. I think we have a chance."

Duce pointed to the other side of the clearing. "I guess we're about to find out, because the other team has arrived."

Giving quick direction, Adam summed up the strategy and gave a brief pep talk. "We're going to win this because of their overconfidence. They've never seen a team like us. Working together we're going to kick ass. Spread out and keep your bola behind your back. We walk up as a unified force and take our shot before they overpower us. Once you have them on the ground, grab their bound legs and drag them behind their line."

K-Eleven stood at the center line. "On three we go." He laughed as he glanced at the more experienced team. "Then we enjoy our feast." He raised his hand, counted to three, then dropped it swiftly. "Go!"

Separated by about thirty feet, the opposing teams ran toward each other. Adam could see the opponent's mouths gape and eyes widen as Alpha squad spun their weapons as they charged. In a barrage, the bolas were thrown, with six adversaries falling. Adam grabbed the sinewy homemade twine now around his target's legs, and dragged him as fast as he could to the disqualification zone, the same as the other five who had taken down their opposite number. He was amazed at the accuracy of the clones who had never even heard of this weapon until a few minutes ago.

With his man down and out, he sprinted and grabbed a large rock, handing it to Z. "Smash the head of the first one that tries to get up!" He glared at the captured. "You know what he's capable of because he's just like you. I wouldn't test his aim."

Duce called out. "Help!"

Running fast, Adam and the others who had captured a competitor returned to the hand-to-hand combat underway just yards away. With their nine to four numeric advantage, they freed Duce from their grip, but the remainder of the fight proved to be a fierce battle. The remaining special ops trainees were a year older, making them stronger and better trained. Adam's martial arts skills helped even the scales.

One of them charged at Adam and he used the man's momentum to flip him in the air resulting in him crashing to the ground on his back. Directing the action on his team, Adam called out. "I need two to drag him across the line."

A pair ran up, and in the maelstrom of the battle, Adam couldn't tell which teammates they were. There was no time to think about how weird it was as he saw another man in a special ops uniform wrestling one of his men to the ground in a headlock. *Not today, asshole.* He joined the fray, and was immediately jumped from behind, pulling him backwards.

Squaring to his opponent, they traded punches to the face, then Adam used a leg sweep to bring him to the ground. He added another blow to the man's nose, momentarily knocking him out.

He left the man and returned to the effort to free his teammate in the headlock. A fist to the attacker's ear loosened his grip.

"Thanks, Boss."

He recognized Duce's accent and smiled. "Anytime." The fight continued for ten minutes with Alpha squad finally dragging the last of the vanquished across the disqualification line. Victorious, they whooped and hollered, sending up a flock of birds, adding to the cacophony of happy noise.

K-Eleven joined the gathered victors and defeated, his voice questioning. "This has never happened."

Adam and Alpha squad stood shoulder to shoulder. "Because you've never met a team like this." In this moment of camaraderie and victory, he felt conflicted. On one hand, he felt as proud as the day he graduated college for leading this team to a win against more experienced guys in hand-to-hand combat. This was exactly the kind of experience he had been looking for. On the other, he knew he was on a mission, and these very soldiers could be turned against him and the Society in unimaginable ways. He decided to savor the moment and leave those concerns for another time. "Show us the pizza and burgers, we're starved!"

K-Eleven pointed to a flicker of light through the trees. "It's right over there. I'll take care of things here and join you in a moment."

As soon as the victors walked away in a flurry of high fives and loud voices, K-Eleven helped the defeated team untangle. "Why did you guys let them win?"

They avoided his gaze until one spoke, in seeming embarrassment. "They simply beat us. We didn't give them anything."

"That matched-eyed son of a bitch embarrassed us all." K-

Eleven was steaming. "I bet the general will be pissed when he finds out." He walked to the other side of the clearing and pulled out a walkie talkie, asking to be patched through to the boss. When he got connected, his message was simple. "General, you're not going to believe this. That outsider made us look like fools."

"Tell me everything."

After hearing a blow-by-blow description, the general's reply stunned K-Eleven. "An even better first day than I could have imagined."

CHAPTER TWELVE

News of Alpha squad's success spread fast, as three days later the entire Tiger Platoon was assembled. Adam had learned they all had been defeated in similar exercises on their first day of training, and several now offered him congratulations. His standard response was to share the spotlight. "It was a team effort. Z and Duce had the expertise, I just helped put the plan together."

Lieutenant Ten-One-Twelve, leader of the platoon made up of five squads, invited Adam to breakfast in their jungle temporary base. "The legend of Adam Clayborn has already made its way back to HQ. Everyone's talking about you and what you did. I hear that even the general knows." He seemed to sneer as he continued. "You'll have to do more than win a glorified wrestling match to impress me."

"Lieutenant, I'm here to learn, and to have an adventure, that's all. And so far, the experience has not disappointed." That wasn't the whole truth, but this lieutenant didn't need to know of his investigation, which hadn't turned up anything yet.

Placing his tin coffee cup on the foldable table, the officer replied. "Call me L-Ten." He paused, as if assessing this newcomer with the emerging reputation. "And if you found the last exercise exciting, then you're going to *love* tonight. Tiger Platoon is squaring off against Gator Platoon in a simulation. You and Alpha squad have been through paratrooper training these last few days, and will play a key role in my plan for us to win. Do you think you can handle it?"

Adam couldn't suppress his grin. He knew his life was lacking something, and with this intense camaraderie and regular jolts of adrenaline, he felt energized and challenged. "I won't know if I'm ready until the action starts, but I can assure you I'm fired up. This is exactly what I need in my life right now."

After a day of preparation, K-Eleven went over the plan again with Alpha and Beta squads as their Cessna continued its climb in the night sky. "We'll be landing on the south bank of the river to secure a key bridge. Expect resistance, but follow the plan and the other three squads led by L-Ten will rush through to take their camp, guaranteeing our victory." He held up two fingers, just as the general had a few days ago. "Victory is ours!"

Everyone, including Adam, replied loudly. "Victory is ours!"

K-Eleven gave final instructions as he held up his walkie talkie. "Check in when you're on the ground, and we'll meet up." A red light inside the plane began to blink. "Line up, we go on green."

When the light turned from blinking red to solid green, a gust of wind hit the small plane and Adam felt butterflies in his stomach. *I'm definitely getting an adventure.* One by one, soldiers in front of him stepped into the inky black sky, falling toward earth. When he stepped out, he yelled. "Geronimo!!!"

Almost immediately he knew something was wrong. The wind was much stronger than those in which they had practiced, and he could see the infrared blinking lights of his team through his special goggles spreading out much further apart than ideal. Swirling gusts sent his parachute spinning. *Not good.* That assessment proved correct as his chute was pushed over the jungle past the landing clearing, leaving him suspended by his cords from the treetop canopy.

K-Eleven's voice came over the radio using his code name. "Dingo One down. Repeat, Dingo One down. Transferring command to Hero One, over."

Adam's muscles tensed as he processed the coded message. *K-Eleven is injured and he just transferred command to me.* He messaged back to K-Eleven and the rest of the men now reporting to him. "Sending new coordinates. Repeat, sending new coordinates." He sent a coded message with his GPS location to the team, then pulled his knife to begin cutting the nylon cords suspending him thirty feet above the ground. With the last line cut, he fell, landing with an impact he knew would break most normal human's bones. *Lucky me.*

Almost upon touchdown, he heard a familiar voice. "Damn, you okay?" Duce was beside him in an instant. "That was an insane drop."

Fudging, Adam didn't have time for that conversation right now. "It's not as high as it looked."

Another voice called as Z announced his arrival. "This is all screwed up. We're on the fucking wrong side of the river. We're in enemy territory."

More calls came in over the airwaves, and the situation deteriorated further. Adam confirmed the worst. "K-Eleven is injured and half of us are on the north side of the water and half on the south."

His mind flashed back to the shootout with Liza Howard when three sides were engaged and no one knew who the others were. Without even thinking, a plan formed in his mind. On the radio he issued orders to the ten soldiers on the other side. "Proceed to Times Square. Repeat, proceed to Times Square."

He could hear the confusion in their words. "Repeat. Did you say proceed to Times Square?"

"Ten-Four. Proceed to Times Square." Adam now looked at his eight men. "We've got to go. Set a fast march pace for the enemy's flank."

One by one his soldiers took turns in the lead, clearing a narrow path through the dense jungle in total darkness. At that moment, he understood how their gene editing helped them, and envied their enhanced ability to see in this low light setting. "You guys are doing great. We're almost there."

After an hour of hard travel, they saw their adversary's camp. Adam had switched the radio to play through earbuds, so as not to alert the other side, and he heard an incoming message from his other team. "We've arrived at Times Square. What are your instructions?"

"Wait five minutes, then knock on the door, hard, but don't enter. We'll handle the rest on our end."

In the five allotted minutes, Adam spread his rag-tag team in an arc just past their sentries, with simple instructions. "On my signal make as much noise as you can as we charge their position." He paused. "And guys, make every shot count. Tiger platoon is counting on us."

At the appointed time Adam's decoy team fired their weapons and threw a couple of stun grenades toward the fortified bridge. He watched as the members of Gator Platoon rushed to defensive positions against the decoy team, leaving their backside unprotected. Adam gave the signal to his team, yelling loudly. "Victory is ours!"

The men of Gator Platoon defending the bridge were thrown into confusion, and the rout was on. The electronic guns of Adam's men sounded like real gunfire, but the only real damage they did was to the egos of the defeated as their vests vibrated and a light on their shoulder lit, indicating a simulated death.

His first shot was a direct hit and the targeted soldier turned around in disbelief. "Where the hell did that come from?"

Z took down two others in quick succession. "Losers!" In just a few minutes, the battle was over.

Only one of the soldiers in Adam's command was hit in retaliation, and while a decisive win, the simulated loss of a man under his command affected him. *I hope I never have to experience that in real life.* Shaking off the pang of loss, he called his decoy team. "Come on in boys, the door is open. We did it!"

A rescue team was assembled to cart K-Eleven out of the jungle with what was now known to be a broken leg and had returned when L-Ten arrived. "From the chatter on the radio, I assumed I would find a shit-show in progress. What happened?"

Adam gave a quick debrief, then L-Ten informed them of their prize for winning. "You should find five cases of beer in coolers around here somewhere." L-Ten held two fingers overhead. "To the victor go the spoils, and guess what? Victory is ours!"

Adam raised his voice with the rest of the winning team. "Victory is ours!"

L-Ten watched the revelry begin, then stepped outside the light of the campfire, placing a call. "I need to speak to the general." In a few minutes L-Ten was patched through. "He turned certain mission failure into spectacular success. He's making us look bad."

After hearing all that had transpired, Volkov had a one-word assessment that confused L-Ten. "Outstanding." The general paused for a moment. "I think both he and I have seen enough to advance to the next step. Bring them all back to base tomorrow. It's time for a very important conversation with Adam Clayborn."

CHAPTER THIRTEEN

It had been a magical week for Precious at Camp Nipmuck. Surrounded by a group that was more like herself than any she had ever known, there was no need to keep a protective guard when meeting new people. Two special relationships had blossomed during the week. One was with Jessica, on whom she had developed a crush. It was mostly hand holding, nearly non-stop talking, and every now and then a quick kiss. The other was with Benz, whom she had come to view as the kindred spirit little brother she always wanted. Today, they had gone to the range for extra archery practice. "Thanks for helping me out, Benz. I want to win the gold medal at the competition tomorrow."

He teased. "You just want a certain someone to give you a winner's kiss."

Her cheeks warmed as she considered protesting, before giggling and confessing. "Is that so wrong?"

"Nah, but I've seen you shoot." He wasn't done teasing. "You're going to need a whole lot of practice to even get on the platform for the bronze."

Precious punched his shoulder. "Hey, I don't stink that bad."

"I'm just kidding. You've actually picked it up quickly, believe me, I've seen a lot worse. Let's get started." Taking aim, Precious let the first of her three-arrow round fly downrange. Between shots, Benz gave tips and encouragement. After a half-hour, his assessment was even better. "Not bad, in fact, that was pretty good."

She spoke as they walked to collect her arrows for another practice round. "You're a pretty cool kid, you know. I kind of wish mom and dad..." Suddenly a sharp pain jabbed her shoulder and her hand reached back. "Ouch!"

A scream came from another archer the next lane over. "Oh my God! Are you okay! I'm so sorry!!!"

Benz spun around and saw a white shaft sticking out of Precious' shoulder, right beside the thin strap of her pink summer top, the tip buried under her brown skin. He yelled to the girl who had fired the errant shot. "Run fast! Go get my mother! Now!"

The teen turned and sprinted away, leaving Benz and Precious alone. He took her hand, his voice quivering. "Sit down, my mom will know what to do. You're going to be okay, I promise."

She sat, more mad than hurt. "I know I'll be fine, but you have to make a promise to me...now."

"Sure, sure." His voice quivered. "Anything you want."

Sighing, Precious shook her head. "My mother is going to be so pissed. This was her worst nightmare."

Benz seemed confused. "It wasn't your fault, it was an accident. I'm certain she won't be mad."

Staring hard, she made a demand. "Get behind me and pull that thing out."

Eyes widening, the ten-year-old took a step back. "I don't think that's a good idea. My mom will be here soon and she'll know what to do."

"Benz," She spoke in a stern voice. "Do what I say, we don't have much time. Get behind me and grab the shaft where it enters my skin, and pull hard. I promise that I'll be alright, I'll be okay."

"Really?" His voice shook. "You want me to do that?" He took his first tentative steps behind her.

"Positive." She ordered. "Stop stalling. I need this out before your mother gets here." She could feel his hand on her shoulder. "One good yank should do the trick."

She could feel his light touch and feel his fingers tremble. "I don't think I can do this."

"I need a brave friend right now, and that's you. Take a deep breath and give it a hard pull, got it?"

"Okay, here goes. One, two, three."

She felt a sharp sting as the arrow dislodged, and a little South African slang slipped out. "Eina! That hurt!" Her left arm reached over her right shoulder to the affected area, stopping the bleeding. "You did great, Benz. Don't worry, everything's going to be fine, but you have to promise you'll never tell a soul what happened."

Benz said nothing as Precious heard Becky's shouts. "We're coming!!"

Stephanie, the girl who shot the wayward arrow, looked as pale as whole milk and her words sounded as if drenched in fear. "I'm so sorry. I didn't mean to."

Precious stood up in a hurry, turning her injured shoulder away from prying eyes. "Don't worry, Steph, it looked a lot worse than it was. In fact, it's already stopped bleeding." She made a joke, hoping everyone would believe her. "But I'm keeping this arrow as a souvenir."

The scared girl's shoulders slumped as she let out a huge breath. "Thank God. I thought you were hurt, and I knew I was in trouble."

Becky put her arm around the relieved girl. "You've got to be more careful, right? Now get back to the office and let them know everything is fine down here. No need to call an ambulance."

"You got it, Mrs. Brown."

When Steph was out of earshot, Becky turned to the two of them with a piercing stare. "What the hell's going on here?"

Benz stepped toward his mother with a sly smile. "It's okay, mom. I think she's like me."

Precious couldn't believe her ears, words tinted in disbelief. "You mean you're special this way, too?"

Becky's hand went to her forehead. "More god damned secrets. That's the last thing we need."

CHAPTER FOURTEEN

As the choppers touched down, returning the troops that had trained with Adam to their base, they all headed to their barracks. There was good-natured teasing between Tiger and Gator Platoons as they walked. Adam summed up the sentiment. "We kicked your ass and drank your beer. Let us know anytime you want a rematch, cause we're always thirsty for more." Adam knew something had been missing in his life, and suspected he needed the sense of danger and adventure, but he was caught off-guard by how affected he was by the brotherhood of soldiers. It added an unexpected positive dimension to the experience.

L-Ten approached Adam as he tossed his backpack onto his bunk. "The general would like you to join him for dinner at seven."

"Time enough for a run before I freshen up." An idea struck Adam. *Now that he's gotten to know me, maybe I can get some info from him.* "Hey, want to join, maybe show me a good trail to work up a sweat?"

"Sure." L-Ten laughed, "But with the humidity around here, you can work up a good sweat just walking to the mess hall."

Soon they left the base at a swift pace along a winding jungle path, stopping after a couple of miles beside a gently flowing river. Adam was drenched but pleased he had kept up. "You weren't kidding about the humidity."

The genetically enhanced soldier pointed to the other bank. "I usually take off my shoes and socks, swim over and back, then chill for a few minutes before the run back. Want to race?"

Running shoes and sweaty socks flew in the air as both men hit the water at the same time, with Adam completing the return milliseconds before L-Ten. "I can't believe I beat you!"

Breathing hard, his opponent agreed. "I've never been beaten by anyone who didn't look like me. They must have tweaked your fast muscle twitch response, too."

They pulled themselves out of the water and soon both had fully recovered. There had been something that bothered Adam, and as he had hopped out, here alone seemed a good time to get an answer. "I noticed that everyone calls Rolan 'General' or 'Boss', but never 'Father' or 'Dad.' I've heard him call you guys his sons on several occasions. What's up with that?"

Shaking out a sweaty sock, L-Ten answered bluntly. "Because that's the way he wants it, and it's made clear from the very beginning."

"I don't understand."

L-Ten shrugged. "I think when there were just a few of us, he did think of them as his children, but K-Three, he called him Kaiden Junior, was killed in a commercial airline crash. No foul play, just a bad landing in snowy conditions. It nearly broke him again to lose a son."

"Sounds rough. I've never heard that story."

"Yeah. The general changed after that."

Turning his head, Adam questioned. "How so?"

"We number in the tens of thousands now, and he can't tell one of us from another. On top of that, he sends us into dangerous situations somewhere around the world every day, with some of us coming back in body bags. I think he found it too hard to deal with a son dying hundreds of times a year. He now looks at us as what we are, a test-tube generated, profit-making fighting force."

"So, why continue calling you sons?"

Lacing his shoe, L-Ten spoke without emotion. "It's good marketing."

Adam shook his head in disbelief as he tied his sneakers. "That's jacked up. Are you cool with this whole setup?"

Standing, L-Ten smiled. "It's the only life I've known, and I really do like the esprit de corps with my brothers. It's where I fit in the world. None of us feel anything special for the general, he's just our employer."

"Interesting." The reply triggered another thought. "But some of you do leave. I'm friends with Maddy Blaze and she's dating a guy named Rex DeMan. You know him?"

"You mean ole K-Sixer? Yeah, I know him, a real piece of work."

"Really?"

"Let's just say he proves that genes aren't everything. I had a nice surrogate family and he was raised by the parents from hell. After what they did to him, they got fired from Rolan's program, and the father even went to jail for child abuse. We're identical, yet as different as night and day."

"Wow."

"Yeah, he's a bad apple, especially round women. His M.O. is to start sweet and end violent. We've bailed him out of jail a few times for assault and battery."

"Oh... good to know." *I need to talk with Maddy ASAP.* Ready to change the subject, Adam looked down the trail toward base. "Care to race back?"

L-Ten's eyes darted to the path. "Loser buys the beer."

"You're on!" Adam pushed off his back foot and the two were at full speed in seconds.

They burst out of the woods two miles later in a virtual tie, depending on the stride. In the final few feet, Adam inched ahead as they flew through the open gate. There was cheering from those who happened to witness the finish, just like at the Kentucky Derby. Slowing down, L-Ten put a hand on the victor's shoulder as he caught his breath. "You're the real deal, man. I'd go to war with you anytime."

CHAPTER
FIFTEEN

From his office window, Rolan Volkov watched the conclusion to the race between Adam and one of his sons, he couldn't tell which one, and didn't really care. He mumbled as he watched them walk toward the officer's lounge. "We've seen you think on your feet and we've seen you display your physical prowess. Now we'll test you in a negotiation."

Two hours later he was standing as Adam entered the same dining hall where Rolan and Bree dined a few weeks ago. "I hope you've enjoyed your time training with my troops."

Looking relaxed in his camo uniform, Adam replied. "It was just what I needed. I spent the first part of my life in school, then went directly into the business world. To work as a team with those soldiers has been an experience I'll never forget, and has already changed the way I look at life."

"Good. I've heard similar stories from most of the executives who have been through the program." The general held up a wine bottle, offering to fill Adam's glass, which he accepted. "There's something about the bonding of soldiers in war that can't be fully replicated in a boardroom, no matter the stakes. For men like you and me, we need that adrenaline rush in our lives."

"I didn't realize that until this week, it's been a transformative experience. Thank you for the invitation to participate."

The general held up his glass. "Then let us toast to the next life-changing opportunity."

Adam held up his glass, his squinted brow signaling confusion. "And what opportunity might that be?"

"We eat and drink first, then talk business. Agreed?"

Adam nodded politely. "Fine by me."

A broad smile graced Rolan's face. "Excellent. Brazilian Gauchos have spent the day preparing skewers of local meats. The flavors are incredible."

He waved his arm and a man wearing a hat similar to an American cowboy, except with a flat brim, moved table-side with a barbeque spit stacked with glistening meat. His English was draped in a heavy South American Portuguese accent. "We begin the feast with the picanha cut of sirloin."

Round after round of meats were brought by the table interspersed with servings of cucumber salad, varieties of bread and several more bottles of wine. Adam surrendered after a buttery tender fillet. "No mas. It's all delicious, but I'm stuffed."

Rolan waved away the final gaucho. "We ate and drank like warriors tonight, and now we discuss the future, where men like us make the world a better place."

A waiter carrying a cigar humidor approached the table. He opened the glass lid and offered. "Would you care for a Cohiba?"

Rolan reached for one of the torpedo shaped smokes. "I get these Cuban's from the same family that rolled them for Fidel."

Adam accepted. "Not my usual end to an excellent meal, but it would be rude to turn away such a special treat."

Fine wine served with excessive quantities of food and these smokes completed the mood he wished to create. They were men who enjoyed the finer things in life and played by a different set of rules. Rolan blew out a large plume into the expansive private dining room where they were the only two guests. "The world was made for men such as you and me. Visionaries bold enough and strong enough to change history."

Adam released a cloud just as big as Rolan's. "I'm just trying to do some good while I walk this Earth. I'll leave others to make those kinds of judgments."

"At our dinner in your restaurant, do you remember me saying I had a meeting at the Pentagon?"

Adam's eyes cut toward his host. "Yes. You said something about a contract extension, if I recall."

A sphinxlike smile eased onto Rolan's face. "What if I told you it was more, that it could change the world?"

His stare narrowed and he spoke curiously. "Do tell, general."

Rolan looked straight ahead. "This is top secret, so I need your word that this stays between us."

"You have it." Adam now sounded both cautious and interested.

The general's chin lifted and his shoulders pulled back. "The Pentagon story was just a cover. The money I'm receiving is really being run through a CIA black budget, so there will be complete US deniability." He chuckled as if he could hardly believe what he was about to say. "We're going to take over an entire country."

"What?" Adam turned to face Rolan. "The American government is plotting a coup?"

"I mean, it's not like it's the first time, is it? And Venezuela has been fucked up for a long time. We'll bring stability and the rule of law back to people who sorely need it."

Leaning back and taking another puff on the stogie, Adam expressed his thoughts. "That's just messed up. A lot of innocent people are going to get hurt." A moment of silence passed, then a question followed. "Then you're handing control over to the opposition, right?"

He gave a low laugh. "That's what the CIA thinks, but I have other plans."

The hard stare returned. "What are you going to do? Steal their country?"

The laugh was now loud and full. "I'm promoting myself from General Volkov to President Volkov, all on the US Government's dime. And the best part is they can't do a damned thing about it, because if they go public, it would expose the CIA involvement."

Adam tilted his head. "I'm not sold on the whole idea of stealing a country because it seems a lot like colonization. No, it's *exactly* like colonization." He stared across the room. "But I have to admit, it's bold." He seemed stunned as he summed up his thoughts. "Good luck... I guess?"

With the setup in place, Volkov played his next card. "And what's even better is that you and the Tree of Life Society are going to help me pull it off." He waited for a reaction from Adam, but couldn't detect one.

A few seconds later, Adam turned and spoke words devoid of emotion. "I don't know what you're talking about."

"Huh. Then we'll play it that way, if you insist." Another puff and billowing release followed. "I'm going to make Venezuela the first country to give equal rights to my sons, and... drum roll please...equal rights to all GM people of any kind. That should make your mother and father very happy."

"Equal rights." Adam shifted. "I like the sound of that."

Volkov resumed. "What I want is for you to fight with me and help set up the new government. You have true leadership abilities, and will be an asset in the fight, plus you have credibility around the world. I'll need that PR shield when other governments realize what we've done. Then, when our coup is deemed a success, we take Brazil. That place is almost as screwed up as Venezuela, especially with Paulo Santos as the president. The man's a certified whacko."

After the short outburst denouncing Santos, Volkov returned to his main theme. "Modified people will have half a continent where they can enjoy equality under the law. Every Society child on the planet would be welcome, and with the financial ties they have, the new nation would thrive. Think about what we could accomplish."

Adam twisted the cigar. "And if I don't want to go along with this plan, with this supposed Society of which you speak?"

The general smirked. "I don't know everything, but I've spent a lifetime figuring things out, connecting dots, building a database of names. Tell your father if you're not back here in a week, then I'm moving ahead with the invasion and releasing all the information I have on the Society. When high ranking officials in scores of countries are exposed, it will cause enough havoc in the world to draw most of the attention away from what I'm doing."

Putting the cigar out in the ashtray, Adam turned to him. "I'm sure I don't know what you're talking about, but I'll relay the message to my father."

A self-satisfied grin shot back. "I'll see you in a week." He took his biggest draw yet, then released it in a slow stream, his tone threatening. "And Adam, don't be late to the revolution."

CHAPTER SIXTEEN

The past few weeks had been the best yet between Madeline and Rex. She lounged in the pool at her parent's mansion pondering baby names, their decision to try to conceive making her smile. *I'm glad I gave him another chance.* Her parents came to mind. *They would be so happy at becoming grandparents...and not having to worry about Huntington's Disease, thanks to the edits they made to me.*

Rex called through the open door. "Time to either come in or put on more sunscreen. We can't have your perfect skin fried to a crisp."

"I'll be right there." She couldn't tell if he sounded concerned or mad about something. *It's time for lunch anyway.*

Rex had his head in the refrigerator as she entered the kitchen. "I'll make you a sandwich."

"No." She thought for a moment. "I'm in the mood for a salad."

Turning to face her, Rex slammed the container he was holding on the counter. "Then make it yourself."

Watching him walk away in a huff, she called out. "What the fuck is up?"

He froze in his tracks, then slowly turned toward her. "No matter what I try to do for you it's never enough. You're always second guessing me."

Confused, she pushed back. "What the hell are you talking about? I just wanted a damn salad."

"It's a salad now, but I know it's going to be just like this when we have this kid" His breathing seemed to pick up. "I'll want to discipline the child one way, and you'll try to override me."

"What are you talking about, Rex? Really, I just thought a salad sounded nice on a warm day." Her mind shifted into a higher gear trying to figure out what triggered this outburst. "What's *wrong* with you?" She immediately regretted her word choice.

His face reddened and his voice bellowed. "What's *wrong* with me? What's wrong with me is that I'm letting some genetically modified pussy boss me around like I'm a nobody! I am somebody, and I'm the man of this house. Do you understand!"

His charge at her was unbelievably fast, his fists raised and ready. She tried to get her arms up to protect her face but he landed a blow first, sending her flying across the kitchen, crashing hard on the polished stone floor. Surprised, but now on guard, she sprang up and her martial arts training kicked in as she readied for another possible assault. "Not again, you son of a bitch!"

He picked up the sealed glass container that held the sandwich meat, then threw it at her. It just missed her head, sailing past and slamming into the wall behind, shattering into a thousand pieces. He stormed out the door, but not before issuing a warning. "I'll be back, then we finish this conversation."

Standing alone in the now quiet kitchen, Maddy shook from fear and anger, with glass shards around her feet. She mumbled as she considered her next move. "He's out of his fucking mind. This isn't going to end well."

CHAPTER SEVENTEEN

As soon as Adam's plane was in the air, he placed a call to his father explaining the blackmail warning from General Volkov, setting off a cascade of events, including a virtual council meeting scheduled for the next day. "This is going to get messy no matter how we handle it."

Ansen sounded on edge. "When do you land? We've got a lot to figure out and not much time to do it."

A tone in his ear indicated an incoming call, and glancing, he saw it was Maddy. "Hey, Dad. Can I call you right back? I need to take this."

"Sure. I knew something was up with Volkov and this is the worst-case scenario."

He hung up with his father and took the call from his friend. "We're on the same wave length. I was literally just about to call you."

Maddy's voice choked on the other end. "Help me, Adam. Rex has gone off the rails!"

A surge of anger washed over him. "What's he done to you?"

"He hit me, hard." She sniffled. "He's gone now, just ran away, but

I know he'll be back. As strong and unpredictable as he's turned, I'm scared."

Adam tried to stay calm, not wanting to upset her any more. "First, call the police. They're a lot closer than I am."

"Can you come, please?"

Shooting a glance out the window, he calculated a rough travel time from Colombia to Los Angeles as his heart now raced. "I'm already in the air, but a long way from Cali, at least six hours. Until then, get your gun and make sure the clip is full. The reason I was about to call is I've learned he's hurt other women before."

There was a long silence on the other end until she made a joke. "I really know how to pick'em, don't I?"

A single mini-laugh escaped his lips. "We can talk about your taste in men later. Right now, you need to protect yourself. He's extremely dangerous."

"Just knowing you're on the way helps." He could hear the resolve building in her voice. "Yeah, I know, but that son-of-a-bitch has hurt me for the last time, I guarantee that."

"You call the police while I get this flight plan changed. I'm on my way."

Adam disconnected, then phoned his father, explaining the situation. He knew he needed to be in two places at the same time, but was sure of where he was needed most. Six hours later his plane touched down at a private airport outside of LA, with a black SUV waiting to carry him and his bodyguards to the Blaze family mansion. He had been unable to reach Maddy on the phone, and as they neared, his heart sank. Police cars were everywhere, their blue and red lights flashing, contrasting with the picture-perfect Los Angeles afternoon. Although not particularly religious, he whispered a prayer. "Please God, let her be safe."

He stepped up to the taped-off scene, met by an officer, his heart pounding. "I need to get in there, she's my friend. Tell me she's okay."

The policeman seemed to recognize him. "Yeah, physically anyway." He lifted the yellow tape. "We were told you were on your way." The officer put his hand on Adam's chest and voiced a warning. "I'm giving you heads up, it's bloody in there."

Violent imagery pushed its way into his brain as he rushed to the front door until stopped by another officer handing him a pair of disposable booties to put over his shoes. "Can't be disturbing the evidence."

He complied quickly, then stepped into a scene even more disturbing than he imagined. Rex lay dead, his body contorted in a bloody pool at the base of the grand staircase. Red splatters intermingled with gory hand smudges, painting the wall all the way down the curved length of the stairs. He spotted Maddy across the open space sitting in a dining room chair talking with an investigator, her back to the grisly site. He avoided stepping on any evidence as he made his way over. His heart poured out as he rushed to her in his final steps. "Thank God, you're safe. I've been worried sick."

Maddy jumped into his waiting arms. "It was awful!" Her reddened eyes released another round of tears. "I had no choice. He was going to kill me."

He smoothed her purple hair as the detective spoke. "I'm Detective Harrel, and I'm glad you're here. Ms. Blaze needs a friend right now."

As Maddy cried in his arms, Adam wanted more details. "What happened, detective?"

"Thanks to the security system, we have a recording of the entire event. The short version is that the deceased forced his way in, then repeatedly struck Ms. Blaze to the point that she fell to the ground, apparently passing out. He backed up a few feet, screaming profanities as she lay on the floor, until turning away for a moment."

Maddy took up the story as she stepped back from Adam, her mood seeming to change as the officer described her beating. Her words flew out angrily toward Rex's still corpse. "But I wasn't out, was I? I made a dash up the stairs where I had left my gun, you hot on my heels." She pointed at the dead man. "But I was faster than you thought wasn't I, asshole!"

The detective continued. "He charged at her and she fired a single shot into his abdomen, momentarily dropping him to his knees."

She seemed to be reliving the event as she again yelled at the dead man. "But you wouldn't stay down, would you? No, you came at me again so I shot twice, knocking you back to the top of the steps."

"These clone soldiers really are made differently." Harrel shook his head. "The son of a bitch had enough left in the tank to charge her one more time."

Maddy took a step toward the body, pointing and shouting louder. "So, I kept pulling the trigger until I convinced you to take your rage downstairs!"

"You can see from the blood on the stairway wall that he took the hard way down. Every tumble and spin were recorded."

The thought of that imagery turned his stomach. "Glad I don't have to view it. I've seen enough violence in my life and I don't need to add those images."

Nodding, the detective rubbed his chin. "I get it. There's a few scenes I wish I could delete from my hard drive." Another officer beckoned him. "Look, we've taken her witness statement, but we're going to be here all-night processing the place. Why don't you two get out of here?"

Her pleading eyes locked on his, and they were easy to read.

"Thanks, Detective Harrel. We'll clear out and give you all the time you need." He put his arm around Maddy and pulled her close. "Let's go someplace safe."

Clinging to him, she agreed. "Take me to my cottage in Santa Monica. I may never set foot here again."

CHAPTER EIGHTEEN

Maddy leaned into Adam as their driver made his way to her beach place. No matter how hard she tried to stop it, when she closed her eyes, the violence of earlier pushed its way into her thoughts. "Thanks for getting here so fast, it means a lot."

She felt his arm flex as he pulled her closer, speaking reassuringly. "We'll always be there for each other. That's the deal."

His words felt like a curative balm to her injured soul. "Always."

The SUV stopped and the driver spoke. "We'll do a sweep, just to be sure the place is safe." He returned in a few minutes as another guard kept watch outside the vehicle. "The property is secure."

Adam made an offer. "With Rex and his company gone, you're going to need new security arrangements. I'll leave this team with you as long as you need."

"Please." She wrapped her arms around him. "After what happened, I don't want to be alone right now. Come in, at least for a little while."

"When's the last time you ate?"

With everything that had happened, she had lost track. "I don't know, but it's been a while."

"You're running on pure adrenaline. Let's order takeout."

Maddy nodded as they exited the SUV. "Nothing fancy, though. I want pizza, wings and beer...lots of beer."

Adam smiled as he gave the driver cash and their order, before putting his arm around her, escorting her into her home. "Anything you want."

Since her parent's deaths she had been living in their house, hoping for some closure at the loss of both. Walking in here, the air smelled stale, so she opened the massive sliding doors, letting warm salty beach air flood in. While she called this her cottage, it was actually a big oceanfront estate, overlooking a sandy beach, with a stunning view of waves rhythmically cresting and falling. "That's better."

Adam spied the wine fridge and saw a green bottle. Pulling it out, he made a suggestion. "Maybe a glass of wine until the beer gets here?"

"Abso-freaking-lutley." She glanced down at the red stains on her arms and clothes. "But I need a shower first. Have a glass ready when I get back...and use the big glasses from the top shelf. I'll need some numbing agents tonight."

When she returned, she joined him on the deck, barefoot, having changed into jeans and a Billie Eilish concert tee-shirt. He handed her a full glass as she sat beside him on a gliding two-seat bench. He raised his. "To the weapons training of our youth."

"I'll drink to that." She took a long swallow then shook her head. "Damn. I meant what I said this morning. I really do know how to pick'em. A druggie bass player...a dumb football jock...now this."

"What's important is you're safe, and he'll never threaten you again."

She took another big gulp. "He seemed so normal, so loving in the beginning. I thought I had broken my losing streak." She gazed out over the waves. "Even with all my success, I've had lousy luck with men."

Putting his arm around her, she heard tenderness in his words. "This wasn't your fault. He spent his entire life hiding his damaged soul, and you survived his worst. That just means you're one step closer to finding mister right."

Maddy shook her head as her voice cracked. "I wish my father had edited the gene responsible for how I make decisions about guys...and a lot of other things."

She leaned into him as he answered. "I'm one of the few people in the world who can completely understand. What you've heard about the mistakes I've made in my personal life is only the tip of the iceberg." He took a sip. "Let's make a deal. We get a clean slate, a fresh start, forgetting about all the errors we've made. How does that sound?"

His embrace felt so natural and, in the moment, she realized he was right. He was one of the few people in the world who understood her completely, and wouldn't judge her mistakes. She could be her gene edited self with him, without fear of hurt or rejection. Moving her hand to his chest she could feel his steady heartbeat as she truly relaxed for the first time since the incident with Rex.

They sat in silence for a long time until the doorbell rang and Adam stood. "Ready for some spicy comfort food?"

She chugged her wine. "Bring it on." They ate greasy pizza and hot wings while trading stories from their shared youth as the sun gradually dipped below the watery horizon. The bottles of beer and blue flames of the fire pit warmed her as a new memory flashed. "Do you remember the night when I found out my mother died?"

Even in the low light, she could see his cheeks redden. "I had just told my parents about Kimee's pregnancy, and you offered a joint, and reassurance that everything would be alright. I needed a friend and you were there for me."

Her cheeks plumped as she smiled. "And we shared that kiss..." Her smile grew as she continued, thinking about that part of the night fondly. "I still rate it as one of the best of my life."

His smile looked as big as hers. "I've never forgotten it, either."

She stood, then touched his shoulder as she walked by. "Wait right here." When she returned, she revealed a perfectly rolled doobie. "Care to recreate the moment?"

Adam's wide eyes met hers. "You've just been through a traumatic event. I don't think that's such a good idea."

She bent down and kissed him, and as their lips parted, she spoke in a sultry but forceful voice. "I was there for you back then, and I want you to be here for me now. I know what I want." Lighting the joint, she inhaled deeply, then leaned in for another kiss, exhaling the smoke into his lungs, shotgun style.

Adam seemed stunned as she turned and sat on his lap...and he sounded nervous. "I don't know about this."

Stroking his face, she continued the seduction, wanting a physical release to push away the darkness that nearly swallowed her earlier today. "We're two consenting adults who've felt sparks before." She kissed him again and unbuttoned the top button on his shirt. "You can't tell me you've never thought about it, can you?"

Returning the gesture, his fingers brushed her face as he responded. "You know the answer." He whispered, sounding torn. "I've thought of it often, but are you sure? Tonight? After what you've been through?"

His touch triggered a rush of emotions in her as the next button was undone. "That's exactly why I want to be together tonight. Distraction has always helped me cope when bad things happen." She took another toke, then again kissed him, gently exhaling to share the oncoming high.

He looked deeply into her famous, genetically edited emerald green eyes. "Would we be making one more mistake we'll regret later?"

Feeling the buzz crawling up her spine and into her brain, she smiled seductively, then batted her eyes. "Maybe, but you're not listening." She spoke slowly. "*This* is what I want tonight."

No more words were spoken as his resistance faded away like the outgoing tide.

CHAPTER NINETEEN

Another week had flown by at Camp Nipmuck, which usually brought a feeling of satisfaction to Becky Brown, but this week was different. It meant that Lesedi and Elna would be arriving to pick up Precious. What she had learned about Precious was startling, but what really concerned her was what Precious now knew about Benz. *One slip from that girl's mouth and our life changes, forever. All our lives. I can see the headlines, 'WAGE founder's hidden secret.' Our business and livelihood would be ruined.*

She leaned against the kitchen counter, lost in thought. *That's just on our side. Lesedi would blow a fuse when she found out the truth. Who knows what would happen then? Would she disown her own daughter and granddaughter? Probably. But no matter what, the papers would have a field day with all of us.*

Precious and Benz had gone to the stables to get in one more ride before she returned home, leaving Becky and Kelley to review their plan. Kelley gave another worried glance toward the parking area. "When they get here, we talk about how much fun Precious had during the week, just as we would with any high-profile guest."

Snapping out of her worried daze, a nod confirmed Becky was on the same page. "Then I suggest Elna join me for a walk to the stables to get Precious."

A black SUV came into view and Kelley drew in a sharp breath. "Here we go."

Lesedi marched in first, speaking with a lilt. "Where's my grand-daughter? Your Bibi is here."

"Precious has your drive." Becky faked a smile. "She's down at the stables squeezing in one more ride before heading home."

The compliment seemed to brighten her mood even more. "I know, and I have high expectations for her. Someday she may take my place as the leader of WAGE, leading the world in the struggle to contain the GM stain."

Becky shot a quick glance at Elna, seeing a micro-break in her smile. *I feel your pain at living a hidden life.* "Elna, join me to go tell Precious you and her Bibi are here."

"A walk before our long flight sounds nice."

Once outside the door, Becky broke the ice. "You've done a wonderful job raising her. She's been a delight, and Benz has a new friend for life."

"Thank you. As a mother, you know how much we worry about our children. With the year she's had, I was hoping this would be an experience that would rejuvenate her spirit."

"Oh, it has, I can assure you." The moment arrived to broach the sensitive subject. "But it's not been a drama free week."

Elna's eyes widened as she replied in a worried tone. "What happened? Why didn't you call?"

"Everything's fine... but we need to talk." Becky pointed to a bench beside the path. "Maybe it's best we sit."

Taking her seat, Elna shook her head as her words choked. "Just tell me what happened."

Becky took the frightened woman's hand. "It happened on the archery range, an errant arrow from a klutzy fellow camper." She paused as Elna lowered her head. "Her wound completely healed in an hour." Becky waited for a moment, then reassured the woman. "Benz and I covered for her, and we won't tell anyone."

Raising her head, Elna spoke somberly. "So, you know. Now two more people know the secret that can ruin her life… destroy our family. That's a weight you can't imagine."

Tightening her grip on Elna's hand, Becky confessed. "Yes, I can. Kelley and I carry the same secret. We know it's a heavy burden."

Looking stunned, Elna turned toward her. "Benz? He's a GM child?"

Becky nodded. "It wasn't our plan, but yes, he's special, too."

As if a veil was lifted, Elna put the pieces together. "So that's why you left WAGE and opened this place. You couldn't live with the hypocrisy."

"Yep. That's it in a nutshell. It's been a great life, but we've lived under the same shadow as you. And now Precious knows about Benz." She sighed. "That's why we need to get on the same page. We'll protect your child if you'll protect ours."

The reply was automatic. "Of course." After a few seconds, she added, "But if either of those two children slip up and says the wrong thing to the wrong person, both our worlds collapse."

"Yeah." Becky spoke the cold hard facts. "I haven't figured out how to prevent that. I guess we'll live a day-to-day existence, walking in faith and hoping none of us step on a landmine."

Elna chuckled. "Speaking of landmines, mother would explode if she found out. Her hatred of edited people runs deep, and the embarrassment she would suffer would only magnify her rage."

Crossing her arms, a thought occurred. "Knowing that, why did you choose to go that route, have a gene edited child?"

Leaning forward and putting her hands on her knees, Elna sounded weary. "Same as a lot of women. Years of trying to conceive naturally followed by round after expensive round of in-vitro, egged on by a biological clock about to expire. We were desperate, and took the risk with one of the few doctors who would take on our case." She shook her head. "We were so naïve about how hard it would be to keep this secret, but look at what we have in our life. Precious is a strong, beautiful young woman. Even if I could go back in time, I wouldn't change a thing."

"Kelley and I feel the same way. We didn't plan this life, but I can't imagine living without Benz." She put her arm over Elna's shoulder. "We have to have each other's back for the good of our families, because if your mother finds out it could destroy us all."

CHAPTER TWENTY

Adam had set up his computer in one of the spare bedrooms of Maddy's home to join the video council meeting. When his screen filled with members, he was especially pleased to see two faces, his ex-wife and his father. *Wonder what Ens would say if she knew about last night? I mean, she and I have gotten closer, but we're still divorced. Would she be happy for us, or mad as hell?* He took in a deep breath as the truth came to mind. *I have no idea how she might react, because I really don't know how I feel about it.*

Ansen kicked off the meeting. "I wish I had better news, but I think we're between a rock and a hard place. I sent everyone a backgrounder on what we're facing, and it's not pretty."

Dr. Chavez spoke first. "Do you think Volkov knows what he claims about the society?"

Adam could sense tension in his father's reply. "Based on my research, I believe it is more probable than not, and we all know how bad that is."

Ensley chimed in next. "And his blackmail demand? What are your thoughts on Adam returning?"

Maybe she still has feelings for me… Stop! Don't be stupid. Get those thoughts out of your head and respond to her. "I don't think we have a lot of choice in the matter if we want to avoid Volkov outing the society. If anyone has a better idea, I'm listening."

There was momentary silence on the call, which didn't surprise him at all. Finally, his father spoke. "I'm still working the problem, but so far, I haven't found any leverage to flip the script. An assassination attempt would be nearly impossible as Volkov is on a fortified base surrounded by trained soldiers. Right now, he holds all the trump cards."

Master Fong turned the equation around. "Then we should consider the ancient words of Sun Tzu, 'In the midst of chaos, there is also opportunity.' What good could come from the turmoil this man is about to unleash?"

Adam had been thinking along the same lines. "The big thing is that he says he wants to create a country where all GM people would have full and equal rights. I'm not advocating taking over a country, in fact, I think it's a terrible idea on so many levels. The people who live there would be going from one dictator to another. But, if we can't stop him, a country where modified people can live without fear isn't the worst outcome."

Gunnar wondered aloud. "Can we trust his word? I mean, he's lying to the US government and seems to have no qualms about it."

"I know his type." Chavez sounded dismissive. "He says what each audience wants to hear. He's a creature of shadows and war, and not to be trusted."

From his limited contact with the man, Adam's gut was telling him the same thing. "Then I *need* to be there to ensure some worse outcome doesn't happen."

Ensley began speaking as Maddy walked to the open doorway of the bedroom Adam was using for the virtual meeting. She had showered and now had her hair up in one towel while another wrapped her body. Stopping, she mouthed the words 'hurry up' as he tried to concentrate on the screen. Ensley filled his ears as Maddy occupied his eyes. *I can't believe she's doing this to me while I'm working on Society business...Wait a minute, yes I can. Maddy wants what Maddy wants, when she wants it.*

He struggled to concentrate as he picked up Ens mid-sentence. ".... whatever you do, come back alive."

He stuttered. "Yeah, uhm, yeah." Maddy finally walked away, making it easier to focus. "I have too much to live for to die in some jungle."

Even though she was three thousand miles away and her image was a two-by-two square on a computer screen, he saw a warm smile he hadn't seen in a long time. "You're darned right you do."

He couldn't help but smile back as his father posed another question, bringing him to reality. "Adam, have you thought of any angles or strategies when you go down there?"

For the moment, he was back to being fully engaged. "It could come down to me trying to take him out, man to man. I'm sure I can do it, but the odds of me making it out of there alive go down drastically. Master Fong, Sun Tzu was required reading in one of my college management classes and I'm reminded of another quote. 'Treat your men as you would your own beloved sons. And they will follow you into the deepest valley.' From what I've observed, General Rolan Volkov either hasn't read these words or doesn't think they apply to him. I plan to exploit his ignorance or arrogance. It won't be easy, but if it works, we could have a peaceful outcome where I don't end up dead."

Ens replied immediately, her flushed cheeks visible even in the small square on his screen. "I'm all for that."

That sounded real... maybe I'm not imagining.

The call proceeded, touching on different contingency plans, but Maddy walked by and playfully stuck her tongue out. His concentration was now totally shot as others covered the diverse angles of how the society would respond if their identity was exposed. Soon, Ansen assigned tasks for follow-up to others, then ended the call.

Adam was shutting the laptop lid when he heard a text message ding. It was from Ensley. *Stop by the city before you go to Colombia. I couldn't forgive myself if something happened to you and we hadn't had a chance to see each other one more time.*

Maddy called out. "Don't make me wait."

"On my way." But before he took a step, he banged out a quick reply to Ensley. *I'll be there tomorrow. Can't wait.*

His phone dinged again. *Then it's a date.*

He looked up at the ceiling, mumbling to himself and the universe. "She used the word 'date'. This is something..." He felt a little like he was cheating on both of them as an inner monologue began. *I mean, it's not like I'm married to either one of them, right? Besides, I'm going to war, and a little pleasure before I risk my life isn't too much to ask, is it?*

Maddy called out again. "Yoo-hoo."

On second thought, if Ens and I were to reconnect and she found out about this, it might be better if I don't make it back. He shrugged. "There's a beautiful woman calling my name. Now's not the time to worry about what might happen." He shoved his phone in his pocket and began walking toward Maddy's bedroom, unbuttoning his shirt as he went, his words sung instead of spoken. "Ready or not, here I come."

CHAPTER TWENTY-ONE

After a second day and night with Maddy, they sat outside in the morning light, watching the waves lap before his scheduled return to New York. He was worried about leaving her alone so soon after what happened. "Hey, how are you feeling, you know, about Rex?"

"I'm dealing..."

Dark sunglasses hid her eyes and he wasn't able to interpret her answer. "What does that mean? I won't leave if you need me here."

She sighed. "Look, we've had some fun, and I enjoyed it, but I think we both know that was all it was." She ran a hand over her colorful hair as she stared at the sea. "Our time together helped me begin to turn the corner on an ugly thing. Now, I need to take the next step...and do it alone."

Relieved that she described the past two days similar to how he felt, he took her hand. "I'm always just a phone call away."

Leaning over, she kissed his cheek. "Thanks. Now don't go getting yourself blown up in some dumb-ass war."

She knew how to make him laugh. "I'll do my best." He turned to face her, saying words from the heart. "Please, promise me you'll take care of yourself. You've been through something horrible, and those kinds of scars take a while to heal."

Now she laughed. "Don't worry, amigo, this is California. I have a therapist on retainer."

She removed her glasses as they stood and hugged. He looked into her eyes, this time as a friend. "I'm leaving my security team with you. And I mean it, call me if you need anything."

With their goodbyes said, Adam returned to the airport, then slept the entire flight back to New York. Waking just before touchdown he was thankful for the luxury of a private plane. His mind drifted and stumbled upon an unusual thought. *My mother's mind would have been blown if you told her this would be the kind of life her baby boy would live.* He took a sip of black coffee, trying to clear the cobwebs. *But it is my life...and it's so crazy I can hardly believe it.*

A quick trip to his apartment gave him time to shower and shave before heading back out the door to meet Ensley at his restaurant. Still in his own head, he mused. *I almost hope I have misread her motive, because the last thing I want to do is screw things up between us...again.* He gave himself a quiet pep talk. "Enjoy the night and let her take the lead. We'll not do anything that's not of her volition."

Paige met Adam and his backup security team as he walked through the doors of Memory Lane. "Everything is set just the way you asked."

Adam nodded. "The champagne?"

"A 1996 Dom Perignon, per your request." Paige turned and led the way to the lofted VIP section.

A feeling of nostalgia overcame Adam as he followed, thinking of Kimee. *Everything seemed so simple back then.* They arrived at the table just in time for him to see Ensley make her entrance with her own set of bodyguards. He smiled as soon as he saw her short sequined take on a little black dress. *Maybe we can reclaim a little of our innocence.*

When Ensley reached the table, she leaned in and gave Adam a kiss on the cheek. "How's Maddy? What happened to her was awful."

His mind went to the bloody scene at Maddy's parent's home. "It was gruesome, and she was a mess, as would be anyone." Keeping a straight face, he told the truth, at least part of it. "But by the time I left, she kind of seemed like her old self. She's going to be alright."

Looking relieved, Ensley turned the conversation to Adam's future as she reached for his hand. "I hope the same for you, that you can go down there and return in one piece."

The warmth of her hand triggered synaptic signals that went straight to the pleasure centers of his brain making him smile, while simultaneously causing him to feel guilty about the time he had spent with Maddy the past two days. He tried to shove the feeling away as a thought came to mind. *Clean slate, remember? It was just two days.* Back on track, he answered Ens. "That's the plan. Like you said yesterday, I have too much to live for." He pointed to the chilled champagne. "Care for a glass of bubbly?"

Glancing, her lips pursed. "Is that a '96 Dom, the same as on our first real date?"

He couldn't have stopped his smile if he wanted… and he definitely didn't want it to stop. "I'm glad you noticed." He waved Brad over to uncork the bottle and serve the vintage sparkling wine. "And unless you want something different, the kitchen is ready to serve the same meal as that night, for old times' sake."

The giggle he remembered so well preceded her reply. "That's so sweet. Truffled bay scallops, right? I don't think I've had them since." The conversation was easy as delicious course after delicious course was served. Intentional or not, they both brought up only pleasant memories, staying away from the hurtful ones of their separation and eventual divorce. When the vodka-chocolate-covered strawberries arrived, she clapped her hands. "You remembered! They're my favorite, and I think of you every time I have them."

Her response made him feel good, especially after all the hurt he caused. "Thanks for inviting me to dinner. I hope this finally moves our relationship from civil back to friendship."

Downstairs, tonight's band started playing a cover version of *Something in the Way She Moves* by James Taylor. She extended her hand. "Let's dance."

They made their way to the floor and his left arm went around her waist as if not a day had passed since their last time dancing at their third anniversary party. There were things he wanted to say, but held his tongue, fearful of breaking the spell he felt he was falling under. He breathed in her perfume and a thousand memory fragments flooded his mind, blocking out the rest of the world. Losing track of time, they floated effortlessly, holding each other until the band took a break.

She held his hand as they headed back upstairs. "That was magical."

A shallow sigh, then a slow smile signaled his relief. "I'm glad to hear you say that. For a moment I feared I might be the only one feeling that way."

She blushed, then changed the subject to his upcoming mission as he poured more champagne from their second bottle. "I wish there was another way. I mean, we've been in some dangerous situations, but tanks, and missiles fired from fighter jets is a whole new level of risk."

"Yeah. And I often think about a comment that Dr. Chavez made when I was young, that I'm not invincible. That's always stayed in the back of my mind."

Ensley sniffed and her eyes glistened, looking as if about to spill. "That's what I'm afraid of, why I wanted to see you again before you leave."

"Hey now, you know better than anyone that you and I are more likely to come back from a fight than almost anyone else on the planet. I'm sure I'll be okay."

"But if something bad happens, I don't want to be stuck with the bad taste of divorce as the way we ended." She reached for his hand again as her voice lowered. "I want happy memories, pleasant memories..." Leaning toward him she planted a soft kiss. "Memories that stay with me forever."

It was all he could do not to immediately wrap her in his arms, instead he stuttered, desperate not to do or say the wrong thing. "I...I... want that too, but, see, I messed things up once before... and I..."

"Adam." She cut him off. "I'm not suggesting we get remarried, or anything like that. I'm just saying that there's a chemistry between us that neither can deny. If something were to happen to you, *those* are the kind of memories I want."

His eyes widened and his brain went again to those two words he had agreed to with Maddy. *Clean Slate.* His mood couldn't have been better as he joked. "Chemistry was always my favorite subject."

She leaned in for another kiss. "I've got a new place. Would you like to see it?"

With his free hand he reached for his glass, raising it, as she did the same. "To wonderful new memories...and clean slates."

Their glasses clinked, then they drained them before heading for the door, arm in arm.

CHAPTER TWENTY-TWO

Ansen sat with Bree waiting for Adam and Ensley to arrive at their estate. "It's nice that they're speaking again."

Bree swept her tawny hair, now featuring a first lock of gray, behind her ear. "I hope it's more than that. I think the world of Ensley and wish Adam hadn't messed it up between them."

"I know, but we can't live their lives for them. Even though they're special, they'll have to figure it out along the way, like everyone else."

The doorbell rang, and Adam and Ensley walked into the living room, hand in hand. Ensley went straight to Bree and the two women embraced. "It's so good to see you again, Mrs. Battle."

"Let's go back to just calling me, Bree, and you're always welcome here." After they separated, Bree reached for Ens again in a second hug, the emotion in her voice palpable. "We've missed you so much."

After a few minutes of small talk, they all made their way outside for a casual dinner under the stars. Ansen proposed the first toast. "To successful missions and safe returns."

After taking a sip, Bree proposed another. "To friends and family. May we always hold each other close." After the obligatory sip, Bree glanced at the two of them, words prying. "You two seem to have mended a few fences."

Blushing, Adam replied. "Mom, really? We've enjoyed a couple of days in the city, but don't get any ideas in your head, okay?"

Shrimp cocktail appetizers were served as Bree answered with a not-so-subtle retort. "A mother can always hope. It's just so good to see the two of you together again...no matter what you call it."

Ansen decided to spare the young people any more interrogation, so turned the conversation back toward the reason for their dinner meeting. "I can't believe you're leaving tomorrow. Are you squared away on the plan?"

With a shoulder shrug, Adam answered. "As much as I can be with so much out of my control. It's a long shot, but there's daylight between the general and his troops. If I can find a way to exploit that, I may be able to change the outcome of the invasion."

"As we discussed, that would be the preferred result."

Adam nodded. "But if that doesn't pan out, then it's on to Plan B. Take out Volkov to prevent a new dictatorship, and hopefully keep the Tree of Life Society shielded."

Bree dropped her fork loudly on her plate. "Is there really no other way?"

Ensley stepped in. "I feel the same, but as part of the council discussion, I know these are the best options from a very short list of choices."

The main course of salmon served on a cedar plank arrived, creating a visual and olfactory draw. Adam smiled. "My favorite. Thanks mom."

Bree dabbed her eyes with her napkin. "I wanted this to be a special night for you." She broke down in tears. "Oh. Adam, I'm so worried for you."

Everyone at the table came to her side as Ansen spoke for all. "This isn't what any of us want, but it's what has to be done."

She protested. "Does it? I mean, I don't want Volkov to take over a country, but I'll take that over losing my son." Then she returned to a refrain she had previously mentioned only in private conversations with her husband. "And would it be so bad if the Society ended? We've accomplished the founder's goal, and then some."

"Mom." Adam answered forcefully. "Perhaps the Society can end someday, but not like this. It would destabilize nations and put a target on all of our backs. I'll gladly sacrifice my life for you, dad and Ens. And think of all the other people you know around the world whose lives would be in immediate danger. Could you live with yourself if Volkov's revelations go public and thousands die?" He spoke with what sounded like finality. "I wish we had other options, but we don't. I'm leaving in the morning."

Bree inhaled abruptly, then exhaled loudly. "Sorry, everyone. I know this is what has to happen, but I just want my only child to be safe. Is that so wrong?"

Squatting, Adam hugged tight. "Our family has faced some long odds and managed to survive, and I intend to keep that streak alive." He chuckled. "And the way I hear it, you brought me into this world during a full military-style assault, complete with a missile firing drone. I'll just be continuing a family tradition."

Ansen couldn't tell if his wife was going to break down again, or explode in anger. She did neither, instead she put a hand on Adam's shoulder, her tone serious. "I should ground you for bringing that up." The comment broke the tension as all laughed.

Ansen shook his head. "Technically, all of us were there, if you count Ensley being just days away from being born. We got lucky that night... and I hope that luck goes with Adam tomorrow."

Dinner continued with small talk on much lighter topics until Adam announced that it was time to leave. "We need to head back to the city. I haven't finished packing." He hugged both of his parents, making them a promise. "I'll be careful, and be back soon."

Bree wrapped her arms around her tall son's neck. "You better be." Tightening her grip, she seemed to barely hold things together. "I love you so much."

Standing on the large front porch, Ansen and Bree watched them get in the back of their SUV and drive away. Ansen tried putting as positive of a spin as possible on the situation. "I know we'll worry, but with his special DNA, there's no one in the world with a better chance to return safely."

"My mind knows that, but all my heart knows is that he'll always be my baby boy, and he can't get back here soon enough."

$$\infty$$

Ens held Adam's hand in the backseat as their driver drove them back to the city. "I really love your mom."

He snorted. "And she really loves you. I think she looks at you and Maddy as the daughters she never had."

"But she loves you the most." Ens rested her head against his shoulder. "I can't comprehend what that kind of love feels like, you know, between a mother and child."

Adam looked straight ahead. "Maybe someday...but it's hard for me to imagine right now."

"Yeah...someday..." Pulling their interlaced hands up, she kissed the back of his as her mind fixed on that idea.

CHAPTER TWENTY-THREE

Adam's plane touched down shortly before noon where he was met by Lieutenant Ten-One-Twelve. "Good to see you, Ten."

The friendliness of the prior week seemed overshadowed as Ten spoke bluntly. "The general is waiting."

On the short open-air ride to Command Central, Adam hoped to get some feel for the vibe of the base. "How's your week been?"

The stare from unmatched eyes was jarring as Ten answered. "We've been at level five alert since you left. I've been told you understand the reason."

"Yeah." Adam slid his ops rated sunglasses from his shirt pocket. "When's D-Day?"

"Tonight." Ten stared straight ahead as the cart neared the main building.

Adam felt a tingle run up his spine as they stopped at the guarded double doors, surprised at how soon the fighting would start. *I thought I would have more time to get my plan going.* He said the one thing he knew to be true. "I'll be right there beside you when the bullets start flying."

The soldier saluted as Adam entered the building where he was met by a soldier he didn't know. "Mr. Clayborn, I'm Lieutenant Colonel K-Ninety-Five-Seventy, but you can call me Lieutenant Yetmis. Please, walk with me to the meeting."

"Yetmis? That's a name I've never heard before."

The officer smiled. "It's the Turkish word for seventy. That's where my surrogate mother lived, and the sound of it is just different enough to stand out around here."

"I get it." Now it was Adam who smiled. "That's kind of hard to do."

Another set of guards stationed on either side of an elevator saluted, and Yetmis did the same as the doors opened. "The general is expecting us."

The elevator swiftly descended, delivering them to a bunkered command center looking like a movie set. Wall size screens currently projected a map of Venezuela. General Volkov was seated at a huge circular table, apparently leading a meeting with his direct report commanders. Seeing Adam and Yetmis enter, he stood and motioned to two open seats to his right. "Please, join us. We're ready to run through the invasion plan one last time."

As they walked to their seats, Adam noted the two concentric outer rings of standing desks, each with a soldier staring at their individual computer screen. They spoke softly into mics and listened through earpieces. Reaching his chair, Adam gave his one-word assessment. "Impressive."

Volkov explained. "It's roughly modeled after Putin's. I toured his command center a few years ago when I signed a big contract with the Russians. It reminds me of my homeland."

Taking his seat, Adam was immediately struck by what he saw, recognizing that other than himself and Rolan Volkov, everyone else at the table looked virtually identical. Without the name-tags in front of each attendee, he would have been hard pressed to distinguish them...that is, until they spoke. The man identified as Colonel Kaw began the overview, his words carried on what sounded like a Filipino accent. "Operation Gideon, in early 2020 was the most recent foreign invasion of Venezuela, and it failed spectacularly. Similar to the Bay of Pigs Cuban fiasco in the 1960's, it relied too much on dissidents and was completely under resourced. It ended before really beginning. We're avoiding both of those pitfalls by using only our soldiers, and to be honest, other than having fighter jets, we're a more lethal force than their entire military."

Volkov interrupted, seeming irritated. "We can't take anything for granted, because in the fog of war, overconfidence gets one killed. I've got a call with the CIA soon, so get on with it and detail the plan."

Chastised, Kaw pointed to one of the large glowing screens showing a map of the country where a black dot now appeared. "Our first objective is to take away their ability to establish air superiority." He pointed to the wall-sized monitor. "The Venezuelan Air Force is small and almost all of their forty fighter jets and helicopters are located at the Palo Negro base."

The general questioned. "And how do we do that with no fighter jets of our own?"

"The element of surprise. The easiest way to put a plane out of commission is to disable it while it's on the ground."

Adam noticed that all of the cloned men in the room nodded in the same cadence. *That's weird...no, that's biology.*

Kaw grinned. "There's a new moon tonight, which will provide maximum cover for our Apache gunships flying below radar, not being noticed by our enemy until too late. If all goes as planned, virtually every combat aircraft in their fleet will be destroyed before the conflict even begins. In thirty minutes, we will own the air."

The matching nods approved of the plan so far. Red dots were now added to the digital map of the neighboring country. "With air superiority established, phase two will commence. These points mark the locations of the other key military bases in the country. We'll parachute in elite teams to each location to begin guerilla harassment. The goal is not to take these bases, but simply confuse our enemy. Because these squads will have no backup, they will be very dangerous assignments."

The corners of Adam's mouth turned microscopically up. *Great. I guarantee Volkov sends me on one of those missions, probably the most dangerous.*

A star was now flashed on the wall-sized map. "With their air force out of commission and every base in the nation under some form of attack, the entire Presidential Honor Guard Brigade will be activated in Caracas. These highly trained soldiers are their best of the best, and serve as protectors and last line of defense for the president. Because of our attacks on the other bases, their calls for reinforcements will likely go unheeded."

Volkov smiled. "And that's when I call our friends in Russia."

What? How is Russia involved?

The colonel's face brightened. "Exactly. With his air force in shambles and no reinforcements to his personal protection detail available, the Venezuelan President will most likely reach out to his favorite super-power friend for emergency help."

The general seemed in a much better mood as the plan continued to roll out. "They came to their aid in the 2019 presidential crisis, and they've helped them avoid oil embargos for years. Putin and I are personal friends and I'll explain that we'll give them an even better oil deal if they simply turn a blind eye this time. Money always talks loudest with the Russians."

Kaw seemed to stand taller. "If all goes as planned, around mid-day tomorrow it will be time… decision time for their leader. Our teams will have taken control of the airport and major ports in the city, so escape is unlikely. Reinforcements aren't coming, and neither are the Russians. He will have to choose between barricading in the Presidential Palace and withstand a siege, or negotiate his surrender."

Volkov seemed to radiate energy as he spoke. "Either way, that's when I arrive in the city. By nightfall Mr. Clayborn and myself will address the world, explaining what just happened, and what will happen in the coming days and years. Our new Venezuelan society will be the most inclusive in the world, inviting all who feel persecuted to join. Viva la Revolution!"

CHAPTER TWENTY-FOUR

Adam had been invited by the general for dinner before deployment around midnight. He thought about the invasion plan as the cart drove through the sticky evening air. *I've got a couple of questions for Volkov, like is he trying to get me killed?*

Entering the dining room tonight, the smells of grilled meat and butter wafted in the air. Volkov stood as Adam approached. "I selected steak and lobster for tonight. I hope that's acceptable."

Adam shrugged. "Can't go wrong with surf and turf."

The waiter came forward as Adam was seated. "Wine, sir?"

"Maybe one glass. I'm jumping out of a plane in a few hours."

With both men having a drink at hand, Volkov proposed a toast. "Za Zdarovje. To health!" The stemware clinked and both men took a drink as a small salad was delivered to the table. "Please, eat. You will need your strength for the hours ahead."

Casting a wary glance, Adam took a bite, then asked a question that had been on his mind since the briefing. "Speaking of health, I know you want me here to help with the media after the takeover is complete, so why have me risk my life in combat?"

Volkov laughed. "It is true that I want your reputation as a PR shield, and I do think your leadership abilities will be useful, but there is a problem."

"Oh? What's that?"

Staring hard, the general seemed to lay it on the line. "It's simple. I don't trust you."

Adam let the words fade into silence before responding. "I see." He took a drink of water. "And how does possibly getting me killed make you trust me more?"

"Don't get me wrong." The general's hand now waved as he talked. "I don't *want* you to die, to the contrary, but I do want blood on your hands. If the world fails to accept our takeover, I want you just as culpable as me. Your reputation needs to be tied to this as much as mine. This is how I ensure that you're really working for our success, and not just phoning it in...or even trying to sabotage what we're doing."

Finished with his salad, Adam pushed the dish aside. Like it or not, Rolan's explanation made sense. "Don't worry about my motivation. Survival is a powerful incentive."

One waiter cleared the dirty plate as another delivered a large platter featuring a filet, lobster tail with butter, and a baked potato as big as a football. Hoisting his glass again, Rolan proposed another toast. "K uspekhu. To success!"

"I'll drink to that."

Between bites, Rolan explained that Adam would be in the platoon led by L-Ten, assigned to take control of the airport. "I want you near the Presidential Palace because you have far more experience in negotiating than Colonel Kaw." His tone turned dark. "He's there to lead the siege if you can't talk the president into surrendering."

The gravity of what he was about to be part of had been building, and weighed on him like a heavy yoke. "I'm about to kill people who have done nothing to me. As a soldier, did that ever bother you?"

"No." He spoke without hesitation. "Politicians decide the goals, and soldiers simply put those objectives into actionable plans. Let go of those concerns; they will only slow you down and trouble your sleep. Focus only on your mission."

Adam knew that the Geneva Convention held that, 'I was just following orders', was not a legal defense for soldiers. He decided not to argue the point with a man who surely knew that, but had chosen to ignore it. Another idea popped into his mind. "But you're not a politician. What gives you the right to do this in the first place?"

Swallowing a mouthful of buttered lobster, the general gave a short reply. "I *will* be a politician by tomorrow night. I'll be the first President of New Venezuela." He laughed. "Do you like the name I have chosen for our country? Hmm? I think it has a certain ring to it."

"New Venezuela..." He rolled the name around in his mind and it had a ring of truth. "If we can achieve our goals, it will be a good fit." While he knew his chances of surviving the invasion were very high, Adam decided to play to Rolan's sense of power over him. The more overconfident he was, the better Adam's chances to turn his men against their leader would be. "That is if I survive the day."

Volkov raised his glass once again. "Tem, kto pogib na voyne, i pust' etogo nikogda ne skazhut o nas." His eyes narrowed as he translated for Adam. "To those who have died in war, and may it never be said of us."

"I'll definitely drink to that."

CHAPTER TWENTY-FIVE

The team assigned to destroy the Venezuelan Air Force at Palo Negro radioed back that their mission was a success. That was the signal for Adam's team to take off from the Anywhere Solutions base, on a straight line for the Caracas airport. Despite the fact that they now had air superiority, they flew with no lighting...just in case. Besides, all of the other soldiers could see in the near dark conditions with their genetic modification, leaving Adam to rely on the technology of night vision in his visor. *I don't know what to think about animal DNA in humans, but I'm getting more jealous by the day of their night vision ability.*

As they got close to their target, L-Ten reviewed their objective over the din of the small plane. "We're taking the control tower first, then securing the perimeter, so expect a firefight. Accept any surrenders, and eliminate all resistance. Questions?"

None were offered as Adam sat between cloned soldiers, rationalizing what he was about to do. *Volkov would be staging this invasion and killing all these civilians even if I wasn't here. On top of that, more lives would be lost, Society lives, if I had refused to do this. There is a chance I might still be able to alter the outcome with a break or two.* After thinking on it a bit, he didn't feel better about what was about to transpire.

The small red light changed to flashing green and all of the soldiers stood, lining up to jump, one by one. When the light went solid, L-Ten shouted. "Victory is ours!"

Shouting with the platoon, Adam could feel the singleness of purpose. "Victory is ours!" One at a time, they stepped into the starlit sky in freefall.

Spotlights from the ground suddenly illuminated and gunfire erupted, aimed upward at his platoon. *So much for the element of surprise.* In quick succession, five of the fifty paratroopers radioed that they had been hit and wounded before even reaching the ground. A quote from an old boxer named Mike Tyson came to mind. "Everybody has a plan until they get punched in the mouth." *We're about to find out how our plan holds up.*

Upon Adam's feet hitting the ground, he got his first answer as L-Ten radioed. "I'm hit! Transferring command to White Eyes."

The new code name for Adam surely left no one doubting who was now in charge. Still, he felt compelled to verify. "Pinnacle, confirm last message of command transfer to White Eyes."

Through choked words L-Ten repeated. "Command transferred to White Eyes." Two heavy breaths preceded additional information. "Per the general's order."

Adam felt his heart rate surge and all senses seemed amplified as he took cover behind the landing gear of a large passenger jet. As bullets whizzed by, he surveyed the terrain. It appeared that the enemy had set up a makeshift barricade at the base of the stairwell door of the control tower. He had read some tactical training material on the flight to Colombia yesterday and he began sending orders over the radio. "All injured personnel, find cover and hold. Repeat, find cover."

Ducking as a stream of fire came his way, Adam waited a moment before his next order. "Z has the lead for Beta Squad. Take position at my ten, behind those passenger ramps. When you get there, lay down suppression fire on their barricade."

"Ten-four, White Eyes." Came Z's sharp reply. "We'll have you covered."

One by one members of Beta squad made their way to Z, and when seven arrived, a steady spray of fire was directed at the enemy. Adam radioed again. "Alpha Squad, on my mark we meet up behind the fire truck on the tarmac." In a break from enemy fire, he gave the order. "Move!"

Sprinting from their individual locations, Adam saw one soldier fall, grab his calf, then get up and limp to cover. Eight men, including Duce, made it to the rendezvous point with Adam. He spoke with pride, seeing the bravery of men he had trained with. "Good job, Alpha." He kept his words light, almost joking. "Now comes the hard part."

He heard a couple of snickers and knew they were ready to follow him. Back on the air, he directed Z again. "I need a ten second heavy burst while we move again, on my mark."

Z's cadence was confident. "Ten-four. On your mark."

Construction had evidently been underway because a bulldozer was parked twenty yards away. Adam pointed, and everyone in Alpha Squad nodded in perfect unison. *That's so weird.* He pushed the thought about the clones away, focusing on their mission to flank the enemy. He radioed Z. "Now."

Leaping up, his team followed him in a dead sprint as Beta squad blasted the adversaries' position. They had almost reached the dozer when he felt a stinging impact to his left shoulder, spinning him around before he fell hard. Duce and another soldier grabbed him under each arm, dragging him to temporary safety.

"You're bleeding!" Duce sounded frantic and wide stares looked down on him.

Adam's right hand had clamped down solidly on the wound and he could already feel the blood flow slowing. *I've got to calm them down.* He moved his arm, barely wincing, then winked at them.

"I'm lucky, it just grazed me."

He pushed through the pain to stand, then glanced toward the enemy. "Now we see how smart they are." He could see relief on their faces as worried shoulders lowered. "We have them flanked, and we're going to make sure they know it. Z, you speak Spanish, right?"

Radioing back, he got the answer he expected. "Affirmative. With a beautiful Argentine accent."

Everyone smiled the same way at his reply. "Alright, then. We're all going to fire on them for twenty seconds, then stop in unison. When it's quiet, I want you to deliver a simple message in their native language... Surrender or die."

Rubbing his left shoulder again, he could tell that the bleeding had stopped. *Good. No time to deal with this right now.* He gave the order to both squads. "On my mark...now!"

Twenty seconds of machine gun fire lit the night sky in a deafening roar, until suddenly stopping. A couple of pot shots were returned, but then came total silence. "Now, Z."

Z's loud voice boomed. "Rendirse o morir."

Seconds passed until firearms were tossed over the barricade. "Nosotros nos rendimos."

Adam chuckled. "My Spanish isn't very good, but I think I know what that means. They surrender." He wiped his bloody hand on his pant leg, then patted those closest to him on the back. "You were all outstanding today." He could feel the tension rise as they seemed to wait on him for a final declaration. He obliged in leading the cheer as loudly as he could, proud of what they had accomplished together. "Victory is ours!"

Both squads answered at the tops of their voices. "Victory is ours!"

CHAPTER TWENTY-SIX

By the time the first rays of sun hit the airport, it was under the complete control of Adam's platoon. The injured were being tended to, and the civilians who ran the control room were sent home. The soldiers they had battled were fed, and now lounged under guard in the small cafeteria at the base of the control tower. Adam had just received orders and relayed them to his men. "Colonel Kaw will be here soon with fresh troops. We'll leave a skeleton crew here and join under his command to find out if the Venezuelan President wants to fight or surrender."

With a little time before phase three of the invasion commenced, Adam pulled out his cell phone and saw that there was still coverage in this part of the capitol. There was an answer on the first ring. "Hi mom. It's me."

"Oh, Adam! We've been so worried."

He could hear the strain in her voice and didn't want to alarm her, even as he massaged his shoulder that had been shot. "Don't worry. Everything is going as planned."

He could hear muffled sounds on the other end, then she came back on line. "Hang on a sec. Your dad wants to talk to you."

Ansen's voice was loud. "I'm putting you on speaker so your mother can hear as well. The news coverage here is all over the place. What's happening?"

Making sure he was still alone, Adam looked over his back toward his troops. "My team took the airport last night, and we're about to join a larger force to complete the takeover. Volkov's plan seems to be working."

"Okay, but you're still thinking about short circuiting his ambitions to become president himself?"

Sighing, Adam replied. "It will be a longshot, but I'm going to try. I think the platoon I'm leading would follow me instead of him, but I'll need to sway a lot more minds in a very short time. Then I'll have to get cooperation from the dissident leader, which won't be easy, but I couldn't forgive myself if I didn't at least give it a shot."

There was a short silence. "We're worried about you, Adam. You don't have to do this."

"I know...and I worry about you guys as well."

He could hear confusion in his father's reply. "Worry about us? What do you mean?"

His hand ran through his hair. "I can't put my finger on it, but the more I'm around Volkov, the less I trust him. His grudge against the Society is personal because of the way his father treated him, and that makes him unpredictable. Like I say, it's only a feeling in my gut."

Ansen's response came quick. "You're the one in a war zone. Take care of yourself and don't worry about us. Okay?"

Gravel crunched behind him. "Alright. Someone's coming, so I have to go. Love you both."

"We love you, too."

With that he ended the call and turned around to see Duce.

"How are the injured?"

"I was about to ask you the same." Duce's eyes locked on his shoulder. "That uniform is pretty bloody."

Seeing the torn material and dried blood running along the length of the sleeve startled Adam, but he recovered quickly. "That little gash sure was a bleeder!" He rubbed stained material between a finger and thumb. "But it closed up nicely. I'm one lucky guy."

With an arched eyebrow, Duce replied. "I'll say. Just like when you dropped out of that tree on our first week of training."

Adam changed the subject, as much to stop this line of discussion as to get a real update. "How are the rest of the guys?"

"Twelve casualties, with six serious. Air evac is on the way for those." He paused. "Three are dead."

The report wasn't surprising, but having people die under his command still shook Adam as he spoke somberly. "We always honor the dead. Let's have a short memorial before the next phase begins."

"What?" Duce seemed surprised. "That's not how we operate. A minute spent mourning is a minute lost in preparation for what comes next. It could cost us another life later today. We grieve when the battle is over."

Putting his foot down, Adam was firm. "Let me be clear, I value the life of everyone under my command. As long as I'm in charge, we'll take a moment to pay our respects for those that have fallen. Got it?"

Duce stood straight at the direct order. "Yes sir. Anything you say, sir. I'll let the others know and get something set up."

"Thanks. Oh, where's L-Ten? I want to wish him well before he's medevac'd out."

"Uh..." Duce lowered his head. "I'm sorry, sir, but he is one of the three that didn't make it."

Adam sensed his cheeks warming, feeling the loss of someone he personally knew in this crazy powerplay by Volkov. At the same time, he realized that as their leader he needed to hold it together. "That's a shame. He was one of the best."

Counting Adam, there were thirty-eight troops in the platoon ready to fight in the next phase. After a final lockdown of the airport control tower, Adam gathered them together and spoke with as much military bravado as he could, for someone whose military training consisted of watching war movies and reading a few books and manuals. "All of you fought bravely and we secured our objective." He paced a few steps before continuing. "But in combat, not all survive to battle again. This morning we recognize the loss of *human* life from this band of brothers."

He had emphasized the word 'human' and watched for a reaction. It was swift and involuntary as they all stood a little taller. "Our brothers fought valiantly as a team, and we will miss the value those *men* brought to our lives."

Not a soldier moved in the stillness of the moment. "Let us never forget their sacrifice nor the *individual* contributions they made in this world."

He felt their stares as much as saw them. *They need to know I see them as distinct, unique people, not just an assembly of interchangeable parts.* "This mission is different from any other in which you've been deployed. When we win, the land upon which we stand will become a home for all...a place where *you* can live free of discrimination. A place where *you* will be able to pursue *your* dreams."

It's time to start the coup against Volkov. "Fight like you've never fought and follow *me* to make those words reality." He could feel their energy building and he smiled as he triggered its release. "Victory is Ours!"

Thirty-seven men never sounded as loud. "Victory is Ours!"

CHAPTER TWENTY-SEVEN

Adam waited for Colonel Kaw in the secured control tower as he watched rented passenger jets filled with troops landing in preparation for a potential final assault. Other similarly acquired non-military cargo planes carried mortars and heavy artillery. *This war is about to get a lot hotter.*

Colonel Kaw strode in, and other than his uniform having a star on his left breast above his service number and name, he looked like every other Anywhere Solutions soldier in the room. His Filipino accent was his most differentiated quality. "I see why the general holds you in such high regard. I was expecting a significantly higher casualty count."

"It's a good team and I care about these guys. Every life matters."

"Of course." Kaw pointed to the north. "Now we shall see if the current president of this country feels the same way."

Adam nodded. "Has the plan changed?"

"No." He looked at his watch. "Our helicopter gunships will

begin strafing the area surrounding the palace in ten minutes, softening any resistance and setting the stage for our arrival."

"Then we contact their president and see if he wants to fight or surrender."

"Exactly." Kaw stared through the windows of the tower and pointed north. "It's fifty clicks to the palace, so we'll chopper in and set up in a command center there. You ready?"

His mind went to the small battle he had just fought, and knew this one would be many factors bigger. His reply expressed a nervous truth. "As ready as I'll ever be."

The advance team radioed back that they had established a secure location for the temporary headquarters, so Kaw and Adam loaded up. The general provided commentary as they flew. "With air superiority established, guerilla teams harassing the other bases and you capturing the main airport, we're on schedule. Our plan is working perf…"

His words cut off mid-sentence as something impacted the helicopter, starting it in a downward spiral. The pilot yelled. "We've been hit! Prepare for impact!"

Adam's vision blurred as the spinning accelerated in their near freefall. He shouted to himself as much as to everyone else on board. "Hang on!" He braced for a very hard landing.

The expectation was a jarring impact and that's exactly what happened. What Adam didn't expect was how loud the crash would be. The sound of twisting metal and exploding fuel roared in his ears as his body came to a sudden stop. On auto-pilot, he began unstrapping and calling out to the crew. "Get out! Everybody okay?"

He heard groans from the front of the broken craft as the pilot answered frantically. "I'm pinned in! Help me!"

"We'll get you out." Adam saw Duce and Z as well as three other soldiers on the craft doing the same as him, scrambling to escape a crashed, burning copter. He turned to the colonel, seeing his head hanging down and not moving. "Help me get him out! He's hurt!"

One of the men stumbled forward and unstrapped the commanding officer as Adam grabbed him under the arms and pulled him to safety. He directed the soldiers. "The pilot's trapped. Help him!"

They rushed back toward the craft whose flames were growing, as he began assessing Kaw's condition. A check of his pulse sent a shiver straight through him and he began CPR compressions. "Come on, you can't die on us now!"

In a few moments the pilot was pulled out and dragged beside Adam, alive and expressing his gratitude. "Thanks for saving me. I thought I was a goner."

Between sharp pushes on their leader's chest, Adam answer. "Every life matters."

Duce checked the colonel's eyes, then his pulse again. He said what Adam suspected. "Yo, sir. You did all you could."

Adam gave one final compression, then pounded Kaw's chest once. "Damn it!"

Sitting back on his haunches, he saw all eyes staring at him expectantly. "How's everybody else? Injuries?"

A chorus of mumbled 'okays' came from the soldiers, and the pilot had made his way to a sitting position. "I think I can walk, but not far."

Surveying their landing site, Adam realized they had crashed in the backyard of a large estate. Several staff members of the manor looked on from a distance. He directed Duce. "Use your language skills. Tell them we're not here to hurt them as long as they keep their distance."

Duce nodded and walked toward the wary group. Adam now turned to Z as the entire helicopter went up in flames. "Did we get the radio out?"

"Yes sir."

"Good. Get on it and get us a ride out of here ASAP." Looking at the destruction, he was reminded of the Mike Tyson quote again. *Everybody has a plan until they get punched in the mouth.* He mumbled. "We just got our first punch in the mouth. Let's see how we handle it."

CHAPTER TWENTY-EIGHT

The rescue helicopter arrived quickly and transported the survivors, and Colonel Kaw's body, to the temporary command center. Adam was escorted inside the makeshift compound and noted the serial number on the soldier's uniform. Instead of using it he asked a very human question. "What's your name, soldier?"

"Bakkar, sir."

"Okay, Bakkar. What's the status here?"

"The general wants to speak to you." Bakkar pointed to a portable phone on a desk formed from a board atop two short columns of concrete blocks.

Adam walked over and picked up the handset. "General."

A gunship flew overhead on another strafing run of automatic weapon fire, making it difficult for Adam to hear the reply from Volkov. "Sorry to hear about Kaw, but as they say in sports, 'next man up.'"

The callousness irked Adam, but he knew now was not the time for that discussion. "I understand. Who's now in command?"

"You met Colonel Tak in our mission briefing yesterday. He's onsite and will handle the military part of the campaign while you'll remain in charge of negotiations with the president."

Glancing around the tarp covered area, Adam looked for a soldier with a star on his uniform as the only distinguishing feature of everyone standing in the shaded area. "I see him. When should we expect you?"

"I have a call with the Russians in half an hour, then I'll check back on progress. I'll remain here until it's time for the formal surrender of their president, or his death."

A smirk formed on Adam's face. *Don't want to put your life on the line like everyone here. Why am I not surprised?* "Hopefully, we can bring that to pass with as little bloodshed as possible."

The reply sounded empty of emotion. "Of course. I'll check back after my call."

As Adam disconnected from the call, Colonel Tak approached, his accent was much less noticeable than Kaw's. "I understand that we are working together."

"Yes." *Sounds Asian. Wonder where he was raised?*

Another strafing run commenced as Tak pointed toward the embattled barricades around the palace. "We are making our point in spades. Let's give it another half hour, then make first contact with them, see if they are ready to talk surrender."

Nodding, Adam expressed hope. "That's what I want. The fewer lives lost on both sides, the better."

"Yes. That's always a possibility, but my experience with dictators leads me to believe that won't happen."

Adam rubbed the back of his neck and sighed. "In that case, I need to grab some food while I have a few minutes."

Tak turned to his left. "There's a supply tent over there. And after the night and morning you've had, you should rest while you can. I'll send for you when it's time for the call."

As if taking a verbal cue from Tak's words, Adam suddenly felt tired as he made his way in search of food, a chair and some shade. Finding all three he ate quickly, then drifted off in exhaustion. A replay of the helicopter crash had just started in his dream when a loud noise and sonic shock hit him simultaneously.

He ended up on the ground with small pieces of debris raining down on him as his ears rang. "What the hell?"

Standing as fast as he could, he was disoriented as he tried to find the command center in a smoky haze of gunpowder. There was a repulsive smell of death mixed in the cloud. He felt cold as he realized that the smoldering pit in front of him was all that remained. *They're dead. They're all dead.*

Duce came running. "Sir! Come with me. We're under attack!"

He ran, following Duce to an area stacked high with sandbag barriers. *Another punch. I'm getting tired of this.* "What happened?"

"A jet dropped a bomb. Looks like we didn't take them all out."

Adam's shoulders tensed. "Like Tak said, they're probably not going down without a fight to the end." Saying the colonel's name, a realization occurred. "We've lost our commander."

Duce looked toward the former temporary field headquarters. "No one survived that blast."

Wonder if THAT would have killed me? Adam shoved the not so hypothetical question aside as he pulled his phone from his pocket and saw that there was no longer service available. *No surprise in a war zone.* Turning to Duce, he gave an order. "Find me a SAT phone or radio. I need to speak to the general."

Duce ran in search of a communications device as Adam became aware of the couple of hundred identical soldiers in the immediate area, all sets of mismatched eyes staring at him. Even in the solemness of the moment, dark humor crept in. *They did say my reputation had grown on the base, and I do kind of stand out in this crowd.* He hopped atop a small stack of sandbags and addressed them, knowing what he needed to say. "We're here to fight for your *individual* rights and I believe with all my heart, this is a just war." That wasn't exactly true, but it was what they needed to hear if his plan was to succeed.

There was hearty applause from the troops, which he let go on until finally ending on its own. With that reassurance, he took a step he hoped would help him in his plan to thwart Volkov. "We've been hit hard this morning, losing both Colonel Kaw and now Colonel Tak. Seems leading you guys is a more dangerous job than expected."

He hadn't intended to be funny when he said those words, but at least half laughed softly, which surprised him. Smiling at their shared black humor, he continued. "Even knowing those odds, I ask that you follow me into battle to deliver equality for you, and equality for all. Are you with me?"

In unison, the reply was strong. "Yes sir!"

"Alright! Get on the radios and let the rest of our teams know of the change in leadership, and be prepared to make some adjustments to our plan. My goal is to win while shedding as little blood as possible. Each one of your lives matters to me."

Another, even stronger response rang out. "Yes sir!!"

He hopped off of the sandbag as Duce came running with a satellite phone. "The general is on the line."

Adam picked up the handset. "General Volkov."

There seemed to be frustration in his voice. "I'm going to need to replenish my leadership team when all this is over."

It was time to let Volkov know of the change. "Then I have good news for you. You'll lose no more colonels in this conflict. In addition to leading the negotiations with the president, I'm assuming full control of the troops here on the ground."

"What?" The general's tone changed from frustration to confusion. "You don't have the experience or the authority." Then his voice changed again, to what sounded like anger. "I'm sending Colonel Estero."

"Do what you want, but the troops are behind me, and I plan to have this wrapped up soon." He paused for a moment to let that sink in before adding a final comment. "I'll wait to press the final assault if you would like to join? It's going to be intense."

The line was silent for several seconds. "Call me when their president is dead or ready to surrender."

"You can count on it." Adam ended the call with an unspoken thought. *I knew you had lost your edge.*

CHAPTER TWENTY-NINE

Adam stood in front of a small group of soldiers who would now serve as his general staff. Duce and Z were included because he knew and trusted them. Bakkar and four others had served Colonel Tak, but like Adam, had been away from ground zero when the bomb fell. He addressed his newly formed command team. "It's time to end this. The longer it drags on, the more incidents like that will happen."

Duce spoke up. "What's the plan, sir?"

Adam glanced toward the presidential palace. "I know it's a symbolic building, but I would trade every building in the city to save one of your lives." He saw what looked like surprise on their faces. "It's time for a dose of good old shock and awe."

Bakkar smiled. "I like the way you think. What do you need, sir?"

"We're done strafing. What kind of air to surface missiles do we have?"

"We have some AGM-65's, but not a lot here in theater." Bakkar glanced at the radio. "Do you want me to request more from home base?"

Putting his hands up, Adam wanted to make a point. "We're doing this fast. No time for resupplying." He rubbed his chin. "We'll just have to do some bluffing. How quick can we have the first four loaded on a couple of Apaches?"

"Thirty minutes max, and sir, those first four are the only four we have here."

"I see. That's where the bluffing comes in. I want every other available gunship surrounding the place and blasting the building while we send those four missiles through the front door. I know they'll be in bomb shelters, but I want to rattle their teeth."

Bakkar smiled. "Got it, sir. They'll be ready."

He walked away with purpose as Adam prepared to continue, then the ground shook again. A few seconds later another explosion sounded nearby. Z pointed across to the other side of the camp. "More bombs."

Duce added information. "From what I can see, they missed most everything this time. Lucky, but they'll scurry away and be back soon."

More determined than ever not to lose another man under his command, Adam spoke. "Then let's end this once and for all. Get us some kind of homemade anti-aircraft system up. We've got to stop this."

In just over twenty minutes the sound of helicopter rotors thumping nearly drowned out Adam's commands to his team. He took in the scene of twenty gunships surrounding the Presidential palace, including the two now armed with two missiles each. He yelled above the roar of the war machines. "On my mark, release hellfire! Three, two, one. Fire!"

The four missiles launched and closed the short distance, crashing through the front façade of the building, then all twenty Apaches began firing their automatic guns. Adam, and every soldier in the forward command center covered their ears as the attack continued unabated for twenty seconds. All firing stopped simultaneously, and the helicopters turned in unison and flew away, leaving the only sound the ringing in Adam's ears. He nodded at Bakkar. "Let's see if we made our point. Get me in contact with their president."

In less than five minutes, Bakkar had established a radio contact with their leader. "We've got him on the line."

"Time for a reality check." Adam picked up the receiver and addressed the Venezuelan dictator. "Mr. President, there has been enough death on both sides today. This ends now, one way or another." While he didn't want to kill everyone in the building, he would if it meant ending the war and stopping the bloodshed while establishing a place his soldiers could call home.

The reply was yelled in what sounded like defiance, but with a clear wobble in the voice. "You can't do this! You can't overthrow a sovereign nation."

"Sir, I understand your surprise, but look outside. We *are* doing this. I'm calling to discuss your personal survival options, and if that fails, I'm bringing that building down on your head. Do you understand?"

There was a brief silence, followed by words clothed in denial. "I am the duly elected president of this proud nation and we will fight to defend our country! The world won't tolerate this! Our allies will stand with us!"

Staying respectful, but direct, Adam stated the facts. "The only friend you have that has the resources to intervene on your behalf are the Russians... and they have switched allegiances. They are now *our* partner. This is not a negotiation." A memory of something he had once heard came to mind. "A wise woman once told me that when the choice is between life or death the decision is easy. Mr. President, I need a decision from you in less than five minutes, or the gunships return, your fate decided for you. Am I clear?"

Resignation was the emotion Adam detected as the president answered. "This evil act will not be forgotten." With that the line disconnected.

Bakkar turned to Adam. "Where did you hear those words about life and death?"

"My mother. She's faced that choice more times than anyone should."

"Huh." Bakkar nodded. "She sounds like a wise woman." He turned back toward the palace. "How smart do you think President Rojas is?"

Adam grabbed binoculars for a closer look at the damage to the building. "I don't know how smart he is, but I do know he's a survivor, not a martyr. He'll call."

The radio tech interrupted. "Sir, you have an incoming communication from President Rojas."

Adam winked at Bakkar. "Told you." He picked up the handset and addressed the leader. "Mr. President, have you made your decision?"

Now, acceptance was the feeling transmitted. "What are your terms?"

A sense of relief washed over Adam, knowing no more lives would be lost today. "First, send a communication to all of your forces ordering them to surrender to us, and if they stand down, none will be harmed."

"Agreed." The president cleared his throat. "And what of my safety?"

"We will be monitoring your communications to your troops. After you have directed them to lay down their arms, a helicopter will land behind the palace, ready to take you to the airport. Once there, you will be flown to Cuba." Adam's voice lowered, just like the time he threatened Becky and Kelley ten years ago. "And if you try anything, we'll burn this nation to the ground and start over."

"You've made your point." He sounded bitter in defeat, delivering a parting shot. "You've won today, but I guarantee you'll get yours. Karma is a bitch."

CHAPTER THIRTY

Bree and Ansen sat close together on a sofa in the den watching Larry Knewell cover the fast-breaking story of the coup in Venezuela. Footage of helicopters firing round after round, with smoke pillars in the background, filled their television screen. She dabbed a tissue at the corners of her eyes. "I'm so worried about him."

Larry had shifted into his newsman, less dramatic voice he used when these types of stories crossed his desk. "Hard facts have been difficult to come by in this rapidly evolving story. We have confirmed that the private army, Anywhere Solutions, has invaded Venezuela from their regional base in Colombia."

A still image filled the screen as he continued. "In a surprising twist, this photo, taken just a few hours ago, shows Adam Clayborn imbedded with the private army troops."

Bree's body startled and her words soared. "He's alive! He's alive!"

Ansen put his arm around her, his words matching her joy. "That's our boy! Thank God!"

The story continued onscreen. "Sources inform us that, at the moment, there's a cease fire between the opposing sides and that negotiations are underway for a quick end to the lightning-speed invasion."

The volume of tears increased as Bree shook. "Hallelujah. This could all be over soon."

Closing his eyes, Ansen said a prayer. "Please, let our boy come home safely."

Larry was introducing a reporter on the ground when the sound of breaking glass broke their concentration on the unfolding action in South America. Ansen jumped to his feet as the sounds of gunfire and startled yells came closer. He grabbed his wife's hand, pulling her up. "We have to go!"

They bolted away from the sound, out the back door of the home, with Bree spying unfamiliar men with guns across the lawn. She yanked her husband to the left. "There are weapons in the stable."

Behind them, voices shouted. "There they are!"

More gunshots rang out, then Ansen fell to the ground, taking Bree down with him. His voice squeezed out words between guttural gasps. "I'm hit...go...take cover."

She ignored him, got up and began trying to drag him toward the open barndoor, just a few yards away. "Stop that nonsense and save your strength!"

The volume of gunfire increased and shots landed in the dirt near Ansen. "Go Bree!" His leg jumped as another round found its target. "Owww. Please! Get to safety!"

Grunting as she struggled to pull his weight, she answered through heaving breaths. "Not a chance. Now shut up, we're going to make it."

The already chaotic cacophony of the early afternoon grew even louder, and those that had targeted them now came under fire, giving Bree a sense of hope. "The cavalry seems to have arrived." After two more backward lunges, she had pulled Ansen inside the half-open doors of the stable where unsettled horse whinnies added to the tension.

Bree scanned her husband's prone body as he lay still, face-down. She spied two wounds, and her mind raced. "They got you in the back and the leg. I've got to find something to stop the bleeding." Her eyes darted, looking for any kind of clean material, finally seeing some towels. "I'll be right back."

Laying with his left cheek pressed to the ground, he called out different instructions. "Forget me, get the rifle from the foreman's office. You have to protect yourself."

She temporarily ignored his instructions. "Not until I get that bleeding stopped. Now, stay quiet."

Once Bree had the towels placed, she looked around for something to secure them, sprinting when she saw the answer. "Duct tape. It's good for everything."

Only after she had the wounds field bandaged did she try to assess his condition. "Can you move?"

Ansen tried to raise up on his elbows, but fell back before even getting halfway. "Sorry. That's all I've got."

Fear washed over her like being hit by a wave in the ocean. *That's not good, but stay positive.* "Okay. You're going to be fine. We'll get some help soon. Just hang in there."

"It doesn't sound like that by the way you're talking." His breathing sounded shallower. "Would you get a gun to protect yourself? Please?"

Nodding, she finally agreed. "I'll protect both of us."

Rushing into the estate foreman's office, she located the small caliber Remington rifle he used to scare away coyotes. "It won't match their firepower, but it will have to do."

Returning to his side, she knelt, gun raised to her shoulder. A nervous joke slipped out. "I thought we had outgrown shoot-outs."

He chuckled weakly. "I was done with them after Nevis, but it seems that's not our fate."

Before she could answer, an Anywhere Solutions soldier burst through the open door. Without hesitation, she fired one shot, striking the assailant in the forehead. He crumpled lifelessly to the ground.

Springing to her feet, Bree grabbed the fallen man's military weapon. Holding the more substantial gun eased her nerves. She spoke as she popped the clip, finding it nearly full. "This is much better."

Ansen wheezed as she stood guard over him. "You were always the better shot."

She smiled at the compliment, but her thoughts were squarely on his wellbeing. "Save your breath, Honey. I'm sure help is on the way."

There had been a small lull in the action, but suddenly the rounds being fired per second ratcheted up quickly, bullets peppering the exterior walls of the stable. Another enemy soldier raced into the barn, seeming to be fleeing, rather than searching for Ansen and Bree. He looked shocked as he began raising his weapon.

Bree released a burst, rather than a single shot, and he dropped beside his identical fellow attacker. "Two down..."

Frantic voices called from outside. "Mr. Clayborn! Mrs. Battle! It's Sedge, where are you?"

His English accent confirmed the voice belonged to the head of security. Bree called out. "We're in here! Hurry, we need an ambulance!"

Ansen's words were slurred. "The police will be here soon. We don't need this kind of attention."

The adrenaline of the moment began to diminish, freeing Bree's mind to consider long range threats. "Please, Honey, stay strong. I'll take care of everything here."

In just a few minutes the sound of sirens found them and paramedics loaded Ansen into the back of the EMS vehicle. Before joining her husband, Bree gave orders to Sedge. "Say as little as possible to the police. I'll be back to deal with this as soon as I know my husband's safe." Even though she had occasionally advocated ending the society, she knew what she needed to say. "This is not the right way for things to end."

CHAPTER
THIRTY-ONE

Adam walked through the shot up Presidential Palace examining the damage he had ordered to be inflicted, broken glass crunching under every step. *It was the right choice to save lives, but I'll not feel totally good with that decision until the place is brought back to its former glory.*

Duce relayed information. "President Rojas' flight to Cuba has left Venezuelan air space."

"Good." Adam turned to the next step in the plan to make a place for equality for all without stealing the country from its citizens. "Where are we in locating the dissident leader, Alejandro Alverez?"

"I think we're getting close. We're interrogating some of the Presidential Guard troops, and they've got a pretty good idea where's he's being held."

Before Adam could reply, Bakkar came running. "Sir, the general is here."

"What?" Adam's eyes widened. "He's not supposed to arrive for another hour. I need more time to get things set in concrete." He bit his bottom lip. "That fucks things up royally." He kicked a big piece of already broken glass, sending it spinning into a wall, shattering loudly. "He's going to be so pissed that I let Rojas leave without the satisfaction of having their president surrender to him. He would have had it recorded to show the whole world his domination, and to feed his ego."

Now it was Bakkar's eyes that widened. "This is not good for any of us. I've seen him angry and it's not a pretty sight."

"Fuck." Adam scuffed his boot on the marble floor. "Let me do all the talking. There's no need for you two to suffer for obeying my orders."

A copter approached and landed behind the palace, and in a few minutes General Rolan Volkov marched in with a protective squad. They strode into the Mirror Room, which had been miraculously spared in the onslaught, and the general wasted no time. "What the hell have you done, Clayborn?"

Adam's gaze was steady as he gave himself a silent pep talk. *Stay cool, things will work out...they always do.* "Doing what it takes to ensure that our new republic gets the international recognition that it deserves. That's what you wanted, isn't it?"

Spit flew as Volkov vented. "This is my plan and my army, and you'll not screw up the dream of a lifetime! Do you hear me?"

Adam nodded, not surprised at how angry the general was, and decided to try to lower the temperature of the situation. "I was doing what I thought best, sir. The less blood we spill the more the outside world will accept what we've done. You brought me in to bring legitimacy to the cause."

The approach didn't seem to be working as Rolan continued yelling. "I knew it, I just knew it! You Society members always think you're so smart and get to make your own rules." He drew in a sharp breath, then took a menacing step forward. "My father acted just like you, always telling me how things were going to be...and I finally showed him, just like I'll show you!"

For the first time, fear entered Adam's assessment. *This son of a bitch is crazy, but just how crazy?* "How did you show him?"

The older man finally calmed, but in a frightening way, his answer spoken low, like a demon claiming a soul. "I put a bullet through him."

That would have been a good fact to know before now. His mind raced toward a new approach. *Let's see if we can bargain.* "I have clearly misjudged the impact of my actions. I know I can double the amount of investment we've been discussing. I'll write the check myself, if I have to."

"You fool. Always hiding behind your money." He pointed and jabbed as he spoke. "I decided to give my old man's precious Society one more opportunity, on the off chance I had been wrong. But in my heart, I knew all of you would turn your back on me, just like he did. Now, a price must be paid for your arrogance and deception."

A chill ran like a zipper up Adam's spine. "What kind of price?"

Volkov laughed in apparent disgust. "Your precious life of course."

Adam's mind flashed back to the day Liza Howard had shot him and he recovered, then to the day Dr. Chavez told him he wasn't invincible. *There's got to be a way.* "Surely there is something else that would be a better price than killing me. I have resources, let's talk."

The general leaned forward, his face morphing into a sneer. "I've got money, and an army." He waved his arm around the elegant room. "And now I've got a country." Next, he spat on the floor. "What I want is satisfaction, and today I've already completed stage one."

"Stage one?" Adam was confused.

"Yes." The sneer twitched into a near smile. "Knowing you might stab me in the back, I had a hit squad sent to the states, ready on my command to exact revenge."

Adam's mind went to a dark place as an ugly thought entered his mind. "Targeting who?"

General Volkov laughed loudly. "Your father, obviously. Cut the head from the snake that is your precious Society."

"No! You can't!!"

Hate filled words returned like thrown knives. "You're too late. He's already dead."

Without hesitation, Adam charged in a rage toward the older man. "You bastard!"

The general's protective detail raised their weapons as the general gave the order. "Fire!"

Adam felt dozens of impacts to his body and his head snapped back with a shot between his eyes. He felt an inky blackness swallowing him as if being pulled into a molten pot of tar. He had one last thought as the darkness fully consumed him. *Dr. Chavez was right, I'm not indestructible.*

General Volkov walked over to Adam's crumpled, bullet-ridden body and delivered a swift kick to the ribs. "I had high hopes for you, I really did. But in my bones, I knew this would be how things ended."

His boot delivered one more blow for good measure. He then pulled out his phone and took a picture of Adam. With a few clicks, the photo was sent. "Because of their arrogance, Mrs. Bree Battle has lost both a son and a husband today."

Volkov spat on Adam's dead body, then directed his gaze toward Duce and Bakkar, staring at their service numbers rather than names on their uniforms. "K-Fifteen, Two-Two-Two, K-Sixteen, Three-Eleven. Get him out of here! Now that the battle is won, round up some wood and the rest of our dead for a victory cremation ceremony."

They answered in unison. "Yes sir."

Volkov spun and walked out of the room letting the world in on his thoughts by quoting Christian scripture. "Let the dead bury their dead." He then added his own philosophy. "Then let the living follow me to a glorious empire."

With the general gone, Duce looked first at Adam's body, then to Bakkar. "One of them saw me as an individual, the other as just a number. I wish we were burning the other one."

Bakkar sighed. "I just met him today, but I feel the same way."

With sagging shoulders, both reached down, one grabbing his hands while the other picked up his feet. As they carried his body, Duce added a final thought. "He's the toughest dude I've ever met. I can't believe he's gone."

CHAPTER THIRTY-TWO

Bree sat in a darkened corner of the surgical waiting room, having nearly filled the small wastebasket with damp tissues. The picture she received from Volkov was revolting, and she had run to the restroom more than once, throwing up increasingly smaller amounts into the bowl. Nasty acid was all that seemed to remain. Between those desperate moments grieving over her lost son, she chanted anxious hopes for her husband's survival. "Please let him live, please let him live."

Ensley rushed into the waiting room and grabbed her former mother-in-law in a bear hug. "I'm here."

Bree's mutual embrace was just as firm, glad to have someone with whom to share her sorrow. "He's gone...my son...your husband. This can't be real."

They held each other in silence, only the sound of weeping moans occasionally interrupting their shared heartache. Ensley's words shook. "I thought we had more time...a lifetime."

"After all the bad things we've lived through, I should be more prepared." Bree's entire body quaked. "But I'm not."

They rocked together as Ensley now bawled. It was a while

before she could even say a few words. "Adam and I had our problems, but we loved each other, and I think that in time, we would have worked things out again."

"I love you like a daughter, and I'll always feel that way."

Taking a half-step back, Ens brushed a tear from her former mother-in-law's face, seemingly pulling herself almost together. "What's the latest on Ansen?"

Fear and agony were added to the sense of sorrow. "He made it here alive, but in bad shape." She sniffed, trying to regain some control over her emotions. "They took him into surgery three hours ago and I haven't heard anything yet."

"That's good." Ens fully released Bree. "That means he's fighting, that he's still alive."

"That's what I'm thinking...when I can think. He just has to be okay."

Ens glanced toward the vending machine. "When's the last time you ate?"

Bree's eyes followed. "It's been a while, but I don't think I could hold anything down."

"You have to keep up your strength, for Ansen. Maybe a few bites?" They walked over and swiped a credit card delivering two bags of chips and two soft drinks. "Let's go sit where it's quiet." Now in a shadowed corner, Ens asked about the scene back at the estate. "What happened? The news reports mention multiple deaths and dozens of injuries."

Bree uttered words as hard and sharp as a high carbon sword blade. "Volkov sent his soldier goons. Our security was caught off guard, and according to Sedge, some didn't make it. If he hadn't rallied our forces, me and Ansen would be dead. Rolan Volkov tried to kill us all." Bree's breath was shallow as she told Ens the rest of the story, Ansen's dried blood all over her blouse. "We heard from Adam this morning and he said he had a plan to thwart him. I guess he tried and failed and that's what *this* is about."

Ensley's hand went to her mouth. "That bastard. The Society is at war, again, and this time facing a real army. I have to get the word out to the other council members." She reached for her phone and fired off a series of texts, then her head snapped toward Bree as full realization dawned. "And one way or another, the Society is at risk of being exposed. This is very bad."

A voice called into the mostly vacant waiting room. "The family of Ansen Clayborn?"

"We're here." Both women stood, then walked toward a scrub attired woman. Desperate words tumbled from Bree's mouth. "Please, tell us that you have good news."

The young woman opened a door. "Dr. McGuire will be with you in a moment. She'll be able to answer your questions."

They sat in a small consultation room, waiting anxiously, until the door opened abruptly. "I'm Dr. McGuire, your husband's surgeon." She wasn't even five-foot-tall, but spoke with the authority of a giant. "Your husband is a lucky man. He lost a lot of blood, and without those towels duct taped tight, he wouldn't have made it."

Bree's cheeks warmed, so happy she had thought to do that. "It was a split-second decision."

"Then it wasn't luck, it was brains." She patted Bree's shoulder. "He's going to need a strong, smart woman to help him on his road to recovery."

Hopeful relief swept over her. "Then he's going to be okay?"

The doctor sat down on the other side of the tiny room, facing the two women, her face drawn. "It's going to be a lengthy path with an uncertain destination. His femur was shattered, and he's the proud owner of several permanent plates and screws."

"But he'll recover?"

Dr. McGuire's hands flexed out. "From that injury, yes, with three to six months healing time and some physical therapy. But he has another, more serious injury."

Although Bree thought she had depleted all of her tears, she was wrong, as they flowed anew. "How bad?"

"One of the bullets nicked his spine, and we won't know the full extent of that injury for some time. It's possible he will have a full recovery, but just as possible he will be partially paralyzed."

The word 'paralyzed' sent a shiver, but Bree focused on the positive. "As long as he lives, that's all that matters." She felt Ensley's arms wrap around her. "When will we know?"

Wide eyes accompanied her reply. "It's extremely unpredictable. Sometimes we know within a few weeks, but it can take much longer to see how much control he will regain. And with his leg injury, it will be a while before he'll be able to do the full range of therapy he might need. It's a real wait and see situation."

Bree reached across and clasped the physician's hands. "Thank you for saving his life. He's my everything, and even more so now."

The doctor stood, signaling her exit. "It's good to see he has such a strong support system. They'll be calling you when he's out of recovery and heading to a room."

She turned and strode out as if on a mission, while Ensley pulled Bree close. "That's good news. He's a strong man and he's going to make it."

The tears fell as Bree looked deeply into Ensley's eyes. "He has to...especially after losing Adam."

It seemed as if hearing Adam's name again triggered a fresh wave of grief for Ensley as she wrapped her arms around herself and sobbed deeply. "No!"

CHAPTER THIRTY-THREE

A throbbing headache was the first thing Adam felt when he realized he wasn't dead. His groan deep, slow and barely audible. "Ohhhhhh."

The next sense triggered was smell, and a single word barely crossed his dry lips. "Gasoline?"

Sound was next to revived, hearing crackles close by, and chants being sung all around. "The bravest among us have fallen. Eternal victory is theirs. Eternal victory is theirs."

"What?" Touch returned, as he felt intense heat near his skin. "What's happening?" Something light and warm fell on his parched lips and his tongue swiped it into his mouth. Tasting it, he spit it out immediately. "Burned snow?"

His mind tried to put the puzzle together, but couldn't. He strained to pry his eyes apart, but they wouldn't open. With tremendous effort he managed to get a hand to his face and slowly rub them, then attempted to open them again, this time with success. He blinked hard, seeing Anywhere Solutions soldiers through a haze of smoke and flame chanting. "The bravest among us have fallen. Eternal victory is theirs. Eternal victory is theirs."

Suddenly, his brain felt as if a bolt of lightning had fallen from the sky, jump starting his sense of self. His eyes darted with purpose, gathering information. The puzzle pieces fell together as if placed by a supernatural force. *They're burning me alive!* The body that moments before struggled to muster enough energy to rub his eyes, now took him to a standing position in one swift motion. He yelled at the top of his lungs. "I'm alive!"

He jumped from the top of the flaming funeral pyre in a forward somersault on the way to the ground, landing hard, but with no pain at all. Hundreds of pairs of identical eyes stared at him as he yelled again. "I'm alive!" He realized there was a chance his plan could be saved if he acted quickly... if they would follow him against Volkov. *They must think I just came back from the dead. I can use this. Let's see what happens.* He shouted as loudly as he could. "Who's with me!"

Eyes as wide as silver dollars stared back, combining with excited murmurs in the crowd. Adam could pick out words like 'alive' and 'impossible'. *It's working.* He implored again. "Who's with me?"

As if under the spell of a risen god, Duce and Z were the first to respond. "I'm with Adam! I'm with Adam!"

Yes! Adam raised his hand in a fist, asking again. "Who's with me!"

Bakkar, and the others who had been with Adam when he was in charge of removing President Rojas, joined now. "I'm with Adam! I'm with Adam!"

Good! It's spreading. For a third time the question rang out. "Who's with me!"

Every soldier in attendance at the cremation service had crowded around, and all answered in unison. "I'm with Adam! I'm with Adam!"

A window in the palace opened outward, and General Volkov's

voice rained down derisively. "What's all the racket about?"

They're all with me! One more time, Adam raised his fist, punching upward with each word. "Who's...with...me!!!"

"I'm with Adam! I'm with Adam!" The response echoed off the white brick walls of the royal building.

The general was two floors up, but close enough for Adam to see well, even in the first hints of twilight. *Revenge is a bitch.* He pointed to the old soldier. "We're coming for you, Volkov!"

Adam saw the window slam shut as he walked to the head of the growing column of identical troops. With the fervor of a revolutionary, he belted out a single order. "Let's seize our future!"

The soldiers charged past him, up a wide set of marble stairs to a broad portico with an entrance door to the palace. Pushing through, the rush continued up the next set of stairs, bursting into the room from which the general had stood moments ago. Adam walked through the throng, finally reaching the front, trying to process the scene. He first saw the dissident leader, Alejandro Alverez, bound and gagged. They had him seated on one of the gilded chairs taken from the ninety-two-seat table in the adjoining dining room. "Mr. Alverez, I see you've met the charming General Rolan Volkov."

He nodded fast and forcefully, trying to speak through the material shoved in his mouth. A muffled, 'Si. Si.' was the best he could do.

Adam turned his gaze toward the general, now with his hands in the air as all of his soldiers, even those in his personal detail, had turned on him with guns aimed. "General Volkov, as the great Mark Twain once said, 'The reports of my death are greatly exaggerated.'"

Looking like he had seen a ghost, he stammered. "How? I saw with my own eyes... You were dead...How can this be?"

Brushing off his questions, Adam got straight to the point, glaring like a million-lumen spotlight. "The last time we were in this room, you told me you had killed my father."

Volkov swallowed hard. "Good news. He might not be dead after all."

Relief registered in Adam's mind but his face remained stone as he spat cold words. "That's great if he's not." He stepped closer, jabbing a finger in the general's chest. "But I'm sure you tried your best to kill him." Breathing in like a bull in the arena, Adam continued. "And I'm damned positive you tried to kill me."

The general stood defiantly as his own soldiers held his arms behind his back. Looking around the room at his troops he gave an order. "I command you to release me and take this enemy into custody!"

Not one fighter moved as Adam laughed in the general's face. "I treat them like individuals. You treat them like disposable genetic property. I bet you don't know the names of any five of them in this room." He glanced around, his eyes landing briefly on several sets of mismatched eyes bearing down on their biological father. Adam spit on the general. "And this is what happens when you treat them as interchangeable pieces."

For the first time, Volkov didn't appear arrogant, but frightened, his face pale and eyes blinking rapidly. He addressed his men. "You can't do this! It's mutiny!" The stares returning offered no change, and realization seemed to sink in as he pleaded. "But I'm your father."

Adam offered an alternate explanation. "Biology alone does not make you a father."

Wide eyes and tight lips met Adam's gaze. "What are you going to do with me? Exile me to Cuba, like Rojas?"

"I'll let your so-called sons decide." Adam looked past Volkov, through the window to the now blazing fire, his anger at this man matching that intensity. "But I do notice we have quite a funeral pyre. I'm sure there's room for one more body."

As if giving permission for recess to begin in elementary school, the troops rushed past Adam and swept up Volkov. A mob mentality seemed to take over as they dragged him. He tried to kick and punch as they made their way down the stairs and into the courtyard, where the flame roared with a voice of its own. The men counted together as two soldiers swung him while he screamed. "You can't do this! I'm your father!"

The soldiers counted together. "One… two… three."

He landed hard on top of the now mature fire, sinking down into the bowels of the raging inferno. The soldiers cheered and hooted.

Adam stared out the window and let the cheering go on for a few minutes before addressing them. "You've seized your ultimate freedom and I share your joy."

The cheering rang louder. "Long live freedom!"

Adam raised his arms. "Stick with me, and soon you'll all taste a new, better life!"

A single word now repeated from the ecstatic mob. "Adam! Adam! Adam!"

CHAPTER THIRTY-FOUR

Bree and Ensley sat close to Ansen's bed, waiting for him to awaken. Seeing him breathing had helped Bree tamp down the anger and depression of what had happened to Adam. Those emotions were temporarily pushed aside with simple anxiety for what would come next for the man she loved. She reassured herself. *He's alive, and that's all that matters.*

A groan came from the bed. "Uuugghhhhh."

Startled, Bree jumped up to be by his side. "We're here, Sweetie. Ens and I are here."

Ansen's eyes pulled apart as he answered weakly. "Where's here?"

Bree replied as Ensley stood beside her. "We're at the hospital. You were shot."

"Shot?" He blinked a couple of times as his eyes seemed to come into focus. "Shot." A statement now instead of a question. "At home, right?"

"That's right, but you made it. You're alive and that's all that matters."

The hand without the IV line moved to his face, rubbing his eyes as he seemed to gain his bearings. "We were watching TV and saw that picture of Adam when it all started."

Bree froze, hearing her son's name and not knowing what to tell her husband. She answered honestly, but her voice involuntarily cracked. "Yes. That's what happened."

Ansen seemed more alert, and his response matched that assessment. "What's wrong?"

Patting his hand, Bree tried to divert. "You were hurt pretty bad, and we need you to focus on your recovery."

"Something's wrong." He squeezed her hand. "Tell me. You have to tell me."

She didn't want to cry yet again, but grief overruled her willpower. "I'm sorry, Honey." She faltered for a moment, then continued. "He's dead. Volkov killed him, and he's the one who tried to kill us."

The hand that had rubbed his face, now went to his forehead as he tried to yell, but with a voice so raspy it sounded like a broken fire alarm. "No!!"

Bree's body convulsed in anguish and tears ran in a torrent. Her phone was laying out of reach on the small table beside Ansen's bed when it rang. Ens reached to hand it to her, but Bree didn't care who it was in this raw time. "Just let it go to voicemail."

With the phone already in her hand, Ens glanced anyway. She gasped as she turned the screen toward them. Her words were a scramble of emotion. "It's Adam."

Bree's mouth opened and a gasp escaped, then she snatched the phone. "Hello?"

"Hi mom."

She wanted to believe, but the photo of Adam's bullet riddled body sent by Volkov, popped into her brain. "It's really you?"

"Mom, it's me. Is everyone alright? Volkov told me he tried to kill you and dad."

Ensley and Ansen could only hear one end of the phone conversation, but it seemed enough as they both peppered Bree. Ens sounded shocked. "He's alive?

Ansen voiced hope. "Our son's safe? Is it true?"

Nodding energetically to both, she replied to Adam. "We saw an awful picture from Volkov and we thought you were dead. I'm so happy, I don't know what to say!"

"I'll explain in a minute, but how are you and dad? Volkov thought he killed you."

Bree glanced down at Ansen's broken body. "He tried, but we survived, though your father is pretty banged up."

An audible sigh sounding of relief came over the line. "I'm so thankful you're both okay."

More tears flowed, but these were of happiness. "We were devastated. We thought we had lost you forever."

Ens tapped Bree on the shoulder. "When's he coming home?"

Bree relayed the question. "Ens wants to know when you're coming home." She spoke with joy. "We all want to see you as soon as we can."

"I've got some business to take care of down here, and I'm sure it will be all over the news. After all, I just helped topple a government, and Volkov is dead. We're safe and so is the Society. I'll stay in touch, I promise."

Wiping her face, Bree still couldn't believe he was alive. "You better. I want to hear from you every day." She choked up. "We thought you were gone, but you're alive. It's a miracle."

"I feel the same way about you two. And tell Ens I'll call her later tonight."

Turning to Ensley, Bree relayed the message. "He'll call you tonight."

That was evidently the final straw, as now Ensley joined Bree in a tear brigade. She spoke loudly. "I'll be waiting!"

Adam answered. "I heard her, mom." He paused. "Listen, there's some important things I need to do today, so I'm going to jump off now. I'll call again soon, I promise."

Soaked in happiness and relief, she said her goodbye. "Okay, we understand. Please take care of yourself."

"I will, I swear."

The call disconnected and Bree leaned in, giving Ansen a gentle hug. "He's alive. Our son is alive."

Ensley joined in with an even gentler hug. "Thank God, he's alive."

Bree thought for a moment about what must have transpired and added an addendum. "And I guess we can thank Dr. Chavez as well."

CHAPTER THIRTY-FIVE

With his call home ended, Adam heard a muffled noise. Turning, he saw the tied and bound leader of the dissident movement, Alejandro Alverez, trying to speak through the gag in his mouth. "Sorry, time to set you free. We have much to discuss."

Once freed, Alejandro was effusive in his thanks. "You saved me from a mad man who was going to kill me. You have my eternal thanks."

"I know exactly how you feel, but we have no more worries of General Rolan Volkov." He gave Alverez a sharp stare. "Our concern is what comes next for this country."

Alejandro stood and cleared his throat. "President Rojas is finally gone, and Volkov is dead. It is *my* responsibility to lead this country."

Adam looked around at the debris strewn room, hoping he might spy a liquor cabinet, but he didn't. Even though he had recovered from wounds that would be fatal to anyone else, his body ached. "Walk with me, sir. Surely we can find some rum around here somewhere. I was left for dead and almost burned alive. I need a drink."

"I was snatched from my home and almost killed by a madman. I could use one as well." Pointing, Alejandro led. "I was shown the presidential bunker once." He chuckled. "Actually, I was taken and personally beaten by Rojas. I know there's alcohol to be found there."

Entering the secure room, Adam was pleased to see a leaded glass cabinet door behind which were premium brands of the preferred drink of the nation. Grabbing a bottle and two shot glasses, both men sat down at a small oval table. Pouring the first round, Adam raised his small glass. "Let us toast to good booze and fruitful negotiations."

Their glasses clinked and the men tossed back the golden liquid. Alejandro swallowed, then questioned, his voice sounding shocked and saddened. "There is to be a negotiation?"

Adam staked out the power position. "We've defeated your nation's armed forces, exiled the president and have you in custody. Of course there will be a negotiation, unless you wish to keep the status quo, which was Volkov's plan. Is that what you want?"

Alejandro sat in silence, arms across his chest seeming to consider his options. In time he reached for the bottle and poured another shot for them both. There was resignation in his reply. "You've made some compelling points, Mr. Clayborn." Both men raised their glasses. "Then let us drink to reasonable men finding reasonable solutions."

Glasses tinged, then Adam leaned forward. *Let's see if he has imagination.* "We have the opportunity to do something special, something the world has never seen, if you have an open mind and vision."

"Sounds intriguing." He fidgeted, not sounding intrigued at all. "What are you proposing?"

At least he understands I'm serious...and he has very few options. "Imagine a nation where everyone was welcome, regardless of

race, religion, sexual orientation, disability…or genetic modification status. Can you see it?"

Alejandro picked up the bottle again, sounding a tad more upbeat. "What you suggest would be…interesting. We must drink
again as I learn more, my friend. May I call you my friend?"

Adam accepted his refilled shot. "Of course. Friendship is a good
starting point."

The Venezuelan gave a weak smile. "To friendship and begin-
nings." Putting the empty glasses back on the table, he questioned, his forehead creased in worry. "My culture is deeply con-
servative, and much of what you have suggested would be very
controversial. If I *could* imagine such a country, how would you
envision overcoming those challenges?"

Adam leaned back, feeling that everything he had done in his
life prepared him for this moment, he stated the basis for his
case. "Money does not solve every problem, but when ninety-
five percent of the population lives in poverty, rapid economic
development buys a lot of good will."

A tilt of the head agreed with that assessment. "Si. I'm listening."

It was Adam's turn to fill the glasses. "Drinking after nearly
being killed makes me philosophical, my friend. Let us drink to
destiny."

Alejandro's head bobbed. "To our destiny, may it be for the good
of my people." With glasses empty again, he pressed Adam. "And
what do you see as your destiny…*our* destiny?"

Musing, Adam spoke words he felt deeply, but would only be
understood by his drinking partner on a surface level. "As the
world's first GM person I feel a sense of history resting on my
shoulders…that I was made to do something important." He
thought about the six-hundred-year history of the Society and
its goal to improve humanity." He sighed reflectively. "And I

have done things that mattered... but I've always felt I needed to do more, that I *had* to do more."

"And you think what we are discussing could fill that void?"

Adam's cheeks felt warm as the corners of his mouth lifted. "I hope so, if we could pull it off. I know it sounds corny, but the more I think about it, the more I believe it does. We could set an example for the world, if we do this well."

"Then we drink again, and set our minds to accomplishing something grand." Alcohol spilled on the table from the sloppy pour, and the toast was slurred. "To fulfilling our purpose."

Leaning forward once again, Adam sketched out the basics. "I can attract more money than you can imagine. We can raise the standard of living in this country substantially, and in short order. There will be money for food programs and for the rebuilding of the nation's crumbling infrastructure. Tens of thousands could be employed almost overnight."

"The previous regimes have run our country into the ground, so that kind of investment would be welcome by everyone." He gave Adam a hard stare as he continued. "As long as there aren't too many strings attached." Alverez paused as if hoping to anchor that point before continuing. "What else do you see in your vision?"

Adam sat, eyes unblinking, as if staring into the future. "Think of a country where people who are different, like me and those soldiers outside, and all kinds of others, would be welcome and have a path to citizenship."

Alejandro's tone turned negative. "I don't think that can happen. The church is very powerful here, and their stands against homosexuality and genetic modification hold a lot of sway."

A grin inched across Adam's buzzed face as he prepared to sweeten the deal. "I'll bet a new president, one who has led the dissident movement for years, would also hold a lot of sway.

He would, of course reside in the rebuilt Presidential Palace, and he could be especially persuasive if he could take credit for the newfound wealth of the country. That kind of leader could change hearts and minds."

Alejandro was still, his red eyes open and fixed for several seconds. "I think your case is getting stronger, my friend." His stare intensified as he made a demand. "But this new president would have to have real power. I'll not sell my country into another dictatorship, even if I were to be the figurehead leader."

"How about this? I foresee a hybrid government in the beginning, with some functions delegated to a freely elected assembly, while others would reside in an executive branch. The new president would, of course, partner with a key advisor."

His eyebrows arched. "Interesting. I could imagine that working." Alejandro then shot a glance toward Adam. "And who might this key advisor be, and what would they control?"

Adam picked up the nearly empty bottle, splashing as much on the table as in the glasses. "Me, naturally. I would be the chief economic advisor and head the unified armed forces, that's non-negotiable. It's a compromise for you, I know, but you would wake up tomorrow in a free country. Imagine that." He dangled the offer as he raised his shot glass. "And you, my friend, would be the President of New Venezuela. We can make the announcement tomorrow... if we share the same vision."

Alejandro picked up his glass with an almost dazed expression. "What else can I say? Viva la Nueva Venezuela!"

CHAPTER THIRTY-SIX

In the month since her husband was shot, part of Bree and Ansen's estate had been transformed into a rehabilitation facility. The weeks had been tough for both of them as Ansen had recovered only a very small amount of sensation and control in his legs. Bree had become her husband's cheerleader, celebrating even the smallest improvement from his daily hours of grueling physical therapy, which wore heavily on them both. She watched the therapist help him maneuver between parallel bars with most of his weight carried by his arms on the horizontal poles, and by belts and bands from above. Every step required intense concentration and massive effort. She whispered to herself. "He's alive. That's all that matters."

He was drenched in sweat after covering a mere four feet. These were the moments that recharged her and she rushed to embrace him as he reached the end for the first time. "You did it! A new personal best!"

An exhausted smile met her praise. "Yeah, and at this rate, I'll be running a marathon by the time I'm eighty."

"Remember, slow and steady wins the race. You've made so much progress."

Hans, the therapist, helped him into his wheelchair, giving Ansen a well-earned break between sessions. Stepping away, he left the two of them alone as he entered the progress into the electronic record.

Ansen wiped his brow with a white gym towel, then looked toward his office. "From what I hear, Ensley's doing a great job standing in for me on council business."

Bree wore a plastered-on smile, seeking to gently guide the conversation. "That's what I hear as well, but you're not supposed to be focused on anything except your recovery. That's got to be your full-time job."

Ansen flipped the small towel over his shoulder. "I know, and I'm trying. It's just that being the patriarch is such a big part of who I am that I feel empty not being involved."

"Sweetie, the biggest challenge of your life is staring you in the face. I know you miss the action, but take a break for a few months. Focusing entirely on your health makes sense."

His head hung and he sounded dejected. "I know. I just feel so damned useless. I mean, I can't get out of bed without help, I can't put on clothes without help." He looked up, meeting her gaze. "Hell, I can't even take a piss without help. I'm helpless."

"It sucks, but the best way to get back to something close to normal is to let others carry the load for a while. You have to pour everything you've got into making as much improvement as possible in this first year. They say that's when the most progress is made."

His lips tightened, then opened with angry words released. "Damn it, Bree! I'm working my ass off and it barely shows! It's hard living like this, and sometimes I wish I had died that day."

His words stunned her and her head shook. "No! You can't think that way. You...*we* have too much to live for. You have a family who really needs you, and your mind is as sharp as ever. I'm not saying this is easy, but it will get better. You have to know that."

He stared at the floor for seconds that seemed like minutes, finally speaking just above a whisper. "Everything you said is true, and I do know it." He looked up, meeting her concerned gaze, the anger from moments ago sounding as if replaced by fear. "Sometimes the road ahead looks like it goes straight up Mt. Everest, and I don't know if I can make it."

Bree patted his leg, speaking with all the love she could muster. "We'll make it together."

Ansen smirked. "You know I can't feel your hand on my leg." He sighed, then his expression warmed to a sly smile as his mood seemed to change yet again. "But a kiss would feel like heaven."

His flirt cut straight to her heart as their lips met. When the long kiss ended, she grinned ear to ear, like she hadn't in a month. "I love you, Ansen Clayborn."

"I love you, too, Bree Battle." His face lightened. "Sorry about that little pity party. I know you're right, I do need to give it everything I've got. That's what it will take to regain as much mobility as I can." His shoulders tensed. "But Society work must go on, with or without me."

"It's gone on for more than six-hundred-years, so I'm certain that a few months sabbatical won't make a difference. Trust your council, after all, you've selected the majority of them."

The shoulders that tensed a moment ago now lowered. "You're a smart woman. Thanks for looking out for my best interests, and for talking some sense into me."

Happy that he saw the situation her way, she hugged him again. "Remember, we're a team. Like at the shootout in Nevis, and the night Adam was born. We have each other's back, no matter what."

"Speaking of back, here comes Hans, and he's got that look on his face."

"You mean the one that gets you one step closer to walking on your own?"

"Yeah, that's one interpretation." His head tilted side to side. "It also looks like the one that's going to crack the whip and make me sweat like a rented mule."

CHAPTER THIRTY-SEVEN

Lesedi Khomalo was Larry Knewell's first guest and simply overhearing her in the hallway, he knew her energy crackled like lightning tonight. He glanced toward her as he awaited the countdown to start the show. He grinned. *This is going to be epic.*

"In five, four, three, two, one." Jared stepped away, the cameras now rolling.

"Welcome everyone, to *Rare Air!*" Larry could feel the air almost vibrate as her intense stare locked on him. "Tonight's first guest is the leader of WAGE, World Against Genetic Engineering. For years the organization has worked around the globe to thwart, or at least slow the spread of human genetic engineering."

He turned to camera two for dramatic effect. "Here in the United States, the group has succeeded in getting laws passed that tax parents who choose to have a genetically modified child at a higher rate. Most recently, they provided model legislation for a national list of all known genetically modified people, functioning similarly to sex offender registries. With just a few clicks you can find out if your new neighbor's child is different."

His gaze went toward his guest. "This week the coalition has initiated its most dramatic step yet, calling for war. It's one thing to tax someone or add their name to a list, it's something else entirely to call for open, armed combat. How can you advocate for that, knowing that innocents are always victims in any war?"

Her words sounded as if hurled by a major league pitcher, fast and hard. "We're defending what it means to be human! A coalition of nations is forming to confront the hostile and unprovoked takeover of Venezuela, led by the first genetic aberration, Adam Clayborn. President Santos of Brazil has reached out for our support as he fears his country could be the next to fall."

"President Santos." Larry said the name slowly, for emphasis. "He's known for his extremist views and has nearly ruined his country's economy. Do you have any qualms about partnering with someone as seemingly unstable as him?"

"No!" There was no hesitation in her answer. "At least he's human, and wise enough to see the threat of a super army being built across his border. What would you have him do? Wait until it's too late to defend himself from their likes?"

Larry hoped to stoke the fire. "But the US government has taken no position on the change in leadership, citing the inclusion of dissident leader Alejandro Alverez as the new president."

The index finger on her right hand jabbed, her dark skin contrasting with her canary yellow suit. "I'm not a US citizen, so I bring a different perspective. Your CIA has been plotting against the former leader for years! Of course they're going to wait and see if this leader is friendlier to American interests. For them, it's all about the money and oil!"

Larry suppressed a smile, loving the fiery words. "Which brings me to another point. All reports are that food aid has been flowing into that deprived country, and jobs are being created at a record pace. The citizens there seem to be supporting the change, at least for now. What gives you the right to interfere with their internal politics?"

A fevered stare met Larry's question. "Because the disease of human modification is spreading in a new and insidious way. From the beginning, those who chose to change what it means to be human have flaunted the law with near immunity. They think they are above the rules of man and nature. Now, they've taken a step too far by taking over a nation, perhaps on a path to take over the entire world!"

Larry raised his hand. "Whoa. That's quite an accusation. What proof do you have?"

She took a quick gasp. "*Those people* now have a real army of their own. At the time of their choosing, they can declare war on their neighbors and begin the process of spreading like a plague across the globe! Someone has to stop them before that happens!"

"But that's all speculation and supposition. Why not let this play out and see what happens?"

Her nostrils flared. "We've already seen what happens when we stand by and wait. There were three babies in the beginning, re-member? They were introduced to the world on your show. We stood by to see what would happen and now there are millions. With their enhanced intelligence and strength, they are taking the best jobs on the planet, already changing our social fabric."

"That's not entirely true." Larry glanced at notes on his desk. "The world GDP has increased at a faster pace than ever, and the poverty rate is at record lows. At best there is a mixed record, but certainly not doom and gloom."

A forceful reply was ready. "Millions of others see it differently and are prepared to band together, putting our money where our mouth is. Armies will be stood up by concerned nations, and WAGE will help defray the cost to those who wish to join the effort, but lack funding. This *is* going to happen."

Larry's brow furrowed. "I get your anger, but what do you say to those innocent people in Venezuela who are not combatants, but whose lives and property will be damaged or destroyed?"

For the first time, Lesedi backed off of her fierce rhetoric. "That will be unfortunate, but it all falls in the category of necessary but regrettable collateral damage. WAGE will pay compensation after the war to those who can prove their claims."

"You sound as callous as those you rail against. You're the one playing God and flouting the rule of law."

The fire returned. "Like they say, Larry, 'war is hell.' The difference is we're trying to save mankind, while their goal is to destroy us all!"

Once again, Larry pushed back. "But Venezuela has broadened human rights protections for all of their population, even guaranteeing the right for same sex couples to marry. Regular people are being helped by this new government."

Lesedi nearly vibrated in her anger. "I've seen apartheid first hand and know of what I speak. When someone in power gives you crumbs of freedom, it doesn't set you free. That's what's happening in Venezuela. The regular people are seeing some improvement in their daily life, but they won't be free. They have exchanged one overlord for another."

Time was running short on this segment, so Larry turned toward camera one and began his wrap-up. "Fifteen years ago, I predicted that there would be both expected and unexpected twists and turns as the world was introduced to genetically modified humans. This latest twist certainly falls in the unexpected category. On one side, people's lives are being improved, but it's the result of a coup led by the first GM human. On the other side, an army is being raised to take back the country, even if it means the death of the very people they claim to be saving. How this will all play out is unknown, but you can be sure that we'll cover it here, on *Rare Air*."

CHAPTER THIRTY-EIGHT

Becky was cleaning up from Sunday breakfast in their home, enjoying the break between camp sessions. Benz was down in the stables feeding the horses as she washed dishes while watching a morning news show. She pointed to the television as another news story about Venezuela played. "Can you believe what Adam Clayborn has done?"

Kelley looked up from her iPad and saw a reporter describing the celebration of New Constitution Day. "He's got balls, that's all I can say. I mean, really, he took over a whole country."

Drying the skillet, Becky clarified. "Sure, it was a gutsy move, but I'm talking about the human rights bills he got passed through their legislature. For the first time, marriage is legal there for people like us. And he got equal protection for all genetically modified people, even those Anywhere Solutions soldiers with animal DNA."

"You couldn't have convinced me of his commitment to human rights that time he kidnapped us." She shivered and ran a hand through her auburn hair. "I still have an occasional nightmare about that."

Becky flashed back to that night and the hatred for him she felt.

She forced out the negative energy with a cleansing breath, then surprised herself. "Me neither, yet that's what he's doing. Maybe he's not such a bad guy after all."

With sarcasm dripping, she replied. "Becky Brown! Are you sick…do I need to rush you to the emergency room!"

She laughed at the good-natured ribbing. "I know, right?" Then her tone turned serious. "I guess that's what ten years and a hundred grand in psychotherapy gets you."

Kelley put her device down. "You've grown so much, come so far. It makes me love you even more."

Becky blushed. "I'm sure I'm a lot easier to live with. I was the angriest woman I knew, back in the day. Jeez, what an idiot I was and what stupid mistakes I made."

Coming to her side, Kelley touched her cheek. "Don't be too hard on yourself. Looking back, we were raised by some angry parents. It's a wonder we're both as sane as we are today."

Succumbing to the emotion of the moment, they kissed and held each other close. Another story came on the news and Becky commented. "Speaking of angry, give a listen to Lesedi."

The head of WAGE was being interviewed about the group's views on the inclusion of protections for GM people in the Venezuelan constitution. "Genetic modification is changing what it means to be human and we must fight against it! We're launching an initiative to persuade like-minded nations to band together and take back that country, by any means necessary!"

"She was even more vitriolic with Larry Knewell a couple of nights ago. I can't watch this anymore." With that, Becky turned the TV off in disgust. "Just think, you and I started that hate group. If they actually gain enough support to start a war, we will be partially responsible for the deaths there."

"No, Becky, don't think that way. We've been gone for ten years. They are responsible for their own actions."

Becky's face pinched. "But we set the trajectory. We're not complete innocents here. People's lives have been ruined, hell, more than a few have even been killed."

Benz raced through the door. "I forgot my work gloves." He took the stairs two at a time on the way up to his bedroom and three at a time on the way down. His sweet voice warmed her soul. "See ya."

His brief appearance lifted Becky's mood. "What a joy."

"Yes, he is." Kelley watched him head back to the barn through the kitchen window. "And he loves those horses and hopes to become a veterinarian someday. We're so fortunate."

That comment reminded Becky of where they left their discussion. "We are for the time being, but what if the world finds out he's modified? That threat always hangs over our head." She paused, then half-joked. "I guess we could move to Venezuela. We could all have full legal protections under the benevolent leadership of Adam Clayborn, unless Lesedi starts a war."

"Becky, don't be so dramatic."

A sharp stare shot back. "I'm serious. I can see the day when we might need to do that. We're one slip up away from being outed as genetic modified parents and have all our names added to the national registry. Moving to a haven like Venezuela might become an attractive option."

Leaning against the counter, Kelley confessed. "Everything you say is true, I just prefer to push those kinds of dark thoughts away. They're too painful to consider."

An idea that Becky had always considered dangerous now seemed almost reasonable, so she gave it voice. "We could stop this, if we wanted to play hardball."

Kelley's head snapped. "What are you talking about?"

Despite her progress on getting her mind in a better place, shades of the old Becky remained, especially the ability to be tough when needed. "You saw how much Lesedi loves her grand-daughter. She can be blackmailed."

"Becky! You can't use a child like that! It's immoral."

Her eyes narrowed. "Think how many lives could be lost if we do nothing. I don't want to see Precious caught in the middle, but if we do this right, we could make the world a better place. Maybe make up a little for the sin of starting WAGE."

Kelley shook her head. "I don't like this, I don't like it at all. There are so many ways this could go wrong and blow up in our face. And it's not just us, we have to think about what's best for Benz."

"I might have to do it, Kelley." She felt desperate. "If a war happens that I could have stopped, I don't know how I would live with myself. Don't worry, I'll contact Elna and keep everything on the DL, but if I have to do this, I will."

Kelley wrapped her arms around her wife and squeezed. "My God, you have certainly changed. I'm scared about doing this, but I'm also so proud of you."

Becky shook her head and chuckled, thinking of all the times she had suppressed her sense of right and wrong. "My therapist told me that sooner or later my conscience would find a voice. I guess this is what she's talking about."

CHAPTER THIRTY-NINE

Ensley had traveled from the city to Ansen and Bree's estate to lead today's virtual Tree of Life Society council meeting. She had been serving as interim matriarch since Ansen's near fatal injuries more than a month ago, and now they were about to discuss extending this temporary situation. Her spirits were simultaneously lifted and crushed when she saw Ansen in his wheelchair. She said, "you look great." While at the same time, she thought, *and you have such a long road ahead.*

Bree smiled as she pushed Ansen close to the desk. "He's working so hard in his PT sessions. It's inspiring to me and everyone else here."

Blushing, Ansen responded to the praise. "Hans should get the credit. He's a master at pushing me to my limit, then inspiring me to come back for more the next day."

Clasping Ansen's hand, Ens spoke from the heart. "This is temporary. You'll be back to your old self soon."

Ansen looked to his wife. "I'm listening to wise advice. For that to happen, I need to focus all of my energy on my therapy, and turn the council reins over to someone who's best positioned to lead in my absence. That's you."

Feeling her shoulders tense, Ens replied. "I'm not as sure as you, but I promise to give it everything I've got."

"I know you will, so let's make it official. Start the meeting."

Ensley pushed the 'Begin Meeting' icon and the screen filled with square boxes containing council member faces from around the world. She stared intently at the square broadcasting from Venezuela. *Adam, I'm so glad you're alive, and I wish you were here.* Pulling her eyes away, she refocused and stared into the camera, speaking to all attendees. "It is with great joy that I'm joined by our patriarch. Thank God you are back with us today."

Applause poured in from around the world. When it finally subsided, he grinned ear to ear. "It's so good to see you all, and I appreciate the well wishes I've received during my convalescence. Your support and kind words have been inspiring."

Adam's reaction was swift. "You're looking so strong."

Ansen flexed his arms. "Six hours of therapy per day has that effect." He put his hands in his lap as he continued. "And that's the point of today's call. To give me the best chance of full recovery, I'm going to need to maintain that kind of intense training for a long time."

Master Fong intoned from China. "I have seen you train, and know that your will is strong. You will overcome this adversity."

"Thank you, Master Fong. I believe that as well. But I also know that with all that is happening in the world today, our Society needs someone who can devote all of their energy to helping us achieve our goals." He took a moment to glance at each square, making eye contact with every virtual attendee. "That is why I propose extending Ensley's interim leadership position for at least six months."

As she had hoped, there were only head nods returning. *Whew.*

The last thing we need is a leadership crisis.

Dr. Chavez spoke next. "That's a smart move, Ansen. I recall the extensive physical therapy your wife endured fifteen years ago recovering from her brain surgery. You will need that level of intensity, and more. I support this decision."

Ens glanced at Bree, who stood stone still, as if recalling those storied, grueling sessions. She kept her feelings hidden, her mind going to a truth about the driven doctor. *Chavez always knows how to set a mood.*

Zadie chimed in next. "With Ensley's leadership role in the GM movement, she is uniquely positioned to keep us informed, and to coordinate activity behind the scenes." She smiled. "Even if she weren't my daughter, I would support her one-hundred percent."

Ens felt her cheeks warm. *Thanks, mom.*

Before she could respond, Adam re-entered the conversation. "And there is so much happening right now, that we will need all the coordination we can get. While things are going well here, there are war clouds on the horizon."

Gunnar questioned. "Adam, I've followed the news closely, but I'm not sure we always get the full story. Can you provide an update on what's happening?"

"Sure." Adam ran a hand through his now shaggy hair. "The past six weeks have been a nonstop flurry of action. Working with President Alverez, we've demonstrated to the people we're dedicated to their well-being. Food has poured in from around the world, and the first infrastructure projects have broken ground, showing everyone that we're doing what we said we would do. It's wearing me out, but I've never felt such purpose in my life."

Instinctively, Ensley looked toward Dr. Chavez, who was nodding approvingly. Her thoughts went to a question she had often pondered. *Was this why we were created?*

Zadie asked a follow-up question. "How are the changes to the constitution being accepted, specifically acceptance of all modified people, including those soldiers?"

"So far, there has been so much favorable press on the positive changes to citizen's day to day lives, it hasn't become an issue. I'm sure it will at some point, but the conditions were so bad that full stomachs and new jobs are trumping any other stories."

Ansen rejoined. "And what about the war rumors you mentioned?"

Adam's tired eyes fell. "That's the biggest concern right now. The integration of the Venezuelan army with the Anywhere Solutions forces is happening, but it's slowed by bureaucracy. We were able to take the country because of the element of surprise, but the combined force is not ready to take on an organized invasion."

Pressing, Ansen asked, "And will the US step in and help?"

A tilt of the head preceded Adam's reply. "The US is in a tight spot. They were shocked by the move Volkov tried to pull, and are still deciding how they feel about the situation I've engineered. They've sent food supplies, but they've signaled they aren't ready to help militarily."

"Adam?" Ensley saw the exhaustion on her ex-husband's face as well as his worry. "Do you think that WAGE group can stir up sufficient outrage to get enough countries to band together to actually start a war?"

His shoulders rose. "That's the sixty-four-thousand-dollar question, isn't it? Their hatred of us is legendary, and their determination seems relentless. It's a real possibility."

That answer made her stomach roll, as it had been doing a lot lately. "Just promise me that you'll be safe."

Ansen added his thoughts. "Same here. The world doesn't need another war." A chorus of agreement filled the virtual meeting space. When everyone had added their voices, Ansen pulled the meeting back to the original topic. "Ensley and Adam are the two people best positioned in the world to stop that potential war. I ask your backing in formalizing support to have Ensley continue as our interim leader. What say you all?"

The response was immediate and unanimous. Ansen sat tall in his wheelchair. "I thank you again for your support of my recovery, and for the unanimous approval of Ensley. The world is on the cusp of so many of the dreams of our forefathers. May fortune smile on what we do."

Reaffirmation poured in as Ensley squared her shoulders, almost literally feeling the pressure of the world transfer to her. *I hope Adam and I are up to this challenge... and any other we will face.*

CHAPTER FORTY

Adam had worked tirelessly to reboot a country that had fallen to its knees under the weight of successive corrupt leaders who placed their own needs above those of the people. So much had been accomplished in the eight weeks since he and the Anywhere Solutions army had toppled that regime, but so much more needed to be done. The biggest item on that agenda was to prepare for a pending war that he hadn't anticipated, and didn't want. The second most important item was to celebrate the success that had already been achieved, and hopefully rally the nation around their defense. To do that a three-day festival was being planned, and he knew who he wanted as the headline act. The call to the artist was a pleasure to make. "Hello, Maddy. How would you like to become the first major American act in Venezuela in over ten years?"

"Adam! It's so good to hear from you. I've been worried."

Just hearing her voice again triggered a surge of positive feelings. "It's been like riding a whirlwind down here, but oh what a ride it's been." He paused, then asked a delicate question. "How are you doing? What went down with Rex was scary stuff."

He heard her take a deep breath before answering. "I had some nightmares early on, then I got some help, like I said I would. The sessions with the therapist have made a big difference, and I haven't had one of those dreams in a couple of weeks."

Her words reassured him. "That's great news. It was smart to see a professional."

"What's up with you, General Clayborn?"

It was still weird to hear his title and he blushed, glad that she couldn't see his reddened face. "You have to come see what we're doing. We're going to have a nationwide celebration."

"Sounds like a party I want to be part of. What are you thinking?"

Good, she's open to the idea. "Next weekend, we're having a festival called, 'Libertad Para Todos', which translates as Freedom for All, and we need a headline act. What do you say?"

"Wow. That's super short notice, Adam. I don't know if I can make that happen. It's a major production to mount a show on that timeline. Can you postpone?"

He sighed in disappointment. "That just can't happen." He paused, not wanting to worry her, but ultimately deciding to go ahead and tell her why. "See, that WAGE group has stirred up anger against what we're trying to accomplish. There's a good chance that a coalition of countries is going to attack in the next several weeks. We need to do this soon, or it will be too late."

"WAGE…" He could hear her anger. "*Those* people have been a thorn in our side for years, when all we want is to live our lives in peace." Her tone changed, now softer. "But I would really like to see you."

"And I really want to see you again as well. I hope the schedule works."

He heard a shuffle on the other end. "I've got a pen and pad to take some notes. If I can pull it off, what kind of venue are we talking about?"

"I'm thinking of you being the final act next Saturday night at Estadio Monumental de Maturín. It's a fifty-two thousand seat outdoor stadium, but with the infield filled, you're looking at close to eighty-thousand."

"Doable… let me get in touch with my crew manager and go over the logistics. It's a big lift to go on the road, especially if it's a one-off like this."

Thrilled, Adam sweetened the deal. "You'll also be the first artist to receive the new National Medal of Performing Arts. You'll be a heroine to the people of New Venezuela."

He could hear a tapping sound as he waited for her reply. "Adam, you know I want to come… to do this…to see you. It's just that I hate making commitments I don't know if I can keep. Besides… I've not been feeling great, and it's going to be a huge challenge to make this happen."

He was jolted as if shocked by electricity. "What's wrong? Are you okay? Tell me you're okay."

"I'm just a little run down, that's all." She paused for a moment. "How about this? I'm seeing a doc tomorrow, and I'll have a chance to figure out if we can get our equipment transported down there in time. I'll give you a firm answer then."

Her answer lowered his concern. "The main thing is that you're okay. You've had so much going on lately, you don't need anything else added to your plate right now."

Maddy sounded upbeat again. "I'm sure I'm fine, don't worry. I really do want to see you again, and if I can make this work, I'll be there. I promise."

"Just hearing your voice has made my day."

"Same here, and besides, I want a new piece of jewelry, and that medal sounds nice. I would be proud for you to pin it on me in front of thousands. It would be another highlight to our crazy lives."

Feeling on top of the world, Adam added. "And I'm sure there will be many more we haven't even dreamed of yet."

CHAPTER FORTY-ONE

For most of his life in the adult world, Adam's daily dress was a suit and tie, or at least a jacket and starched shirt paired with crisply tailored slacks. For the past two months, however, he wore a camo Anywhere Solutions standard issue uniform... and he liked the change. Today he sat at the head of the table of the new combined forces of New Venezuela. "General Jimenez, what's the latest?"

The general walked to a wall map adjacent to the circular conference table. "We have confirmed that Brazil is massing troops along our common border. Analysis also indicates that those forces are being augmented by soldiers and equipment from Argentina and Paraguay, as well as small numbers of troops from former Soviet nations not aligned with NATO."

"And what do we know about their intent. Do they want to flex their muscle as a warning, or are we looking at an imminent invasion?"

Sitting back down, the tilt of his head indicated his response. "It's hard to say. What we do know is the force is formidable, and could very well win in a sustained war."

Adam thought back on the brilliance of Volkov's plan, using the element of surprise to defeat a numerically superior force. That wasn't an option now, so he presented another strategy. "Then we must find ways to convince them that even if a military campaign is successful, the price they will pay will cost more than it's worth."

Duce now served as Adam's right-hand man. "Are you thinking something like chemical weapons as a deterrent?"

Adam shook his head, shocked that it had been offered as an option. As much as he now trusted these men, there was a lot still left to learn about them. "No. The country needs to come out of this standoff with a good reputation, and one way to torpedo that is the use of those kinds of weapons."

General Flores, head of the air force followed up. "We're still getting our fleet back in shape after the takeover." His words seemed to carry lingering anger over his defeat, but those who swore loyalty to the new constitution kept their jobs, and received a raise. He presented an option. "But we can fly sorties along the border to let them know an invasion will be bloody, and won't be easy."

"I like that idea." Adam nodded. "It will demoralize their front-line forces who probably don't want this war anyway." Adam had made sure that President Alverez was part of all war planning and glancing at him, he saw a creased brow. "I sense that you believe that won't be enough."

The president spoke for the first time today. "No, not even close. We're going to need things like economic pressure and other nations coming out as potential allies."

Adam squared his shoulders in agreement. "It's one thing for them to lose ten thousand troops, but quite another to see their economies go into recession, or risk having an even bigger enemy side with us. The risk has to be existential, threatening their regime's very survival."

Alverez spoke what had become a major source of concern. "It would be so much easier to figure all this out if Brazil had a stable leader. Santos isn't called The Mad Hatter of South America for nothing." He bit his lower lip. "We can't change that, so we really need some friends with guns. Do you think the US will side with us?"

Adam shook his head. "They're still trying to decide if they can trust us. While they are glad Rojas is gone and that you're the new president, the wrinkle of the Anywhere Solutions army now being part of the plan has them scratching their head. At best, they will stay neutral."

"Then what are our options, or is war inevitable?"

The answer to that question partly lay with the Tree of Life Society. Adam's involvement with nation building was his doing, and not Society business, but their interests did overlap. How far would they go to help was the big question. "I've got a few aces up my sleeve, but I'll need to draw to an inside straight. That means we prepare for war and hope for the best while I go on a covert diplomatic mission."

CHAPTER FORTY-TWO

Adam's plane touched down in New York and in just over an hour he was at his parent's estate. So much had changed in the two months since he had last seen them. They had been involved in a shootout leaving his father partially paralyzed, and he had been presumed dead. On top of that, Ensley was now the temporary leader of the Society as his father recuperated. He had pushed all emotion aside as he worked sixteen-hour days to set New Venezuela on a better, prosperous path, but the closer he got to their home the more the emotion came to the surface. *I can't wait to see them all.* As soon as the SUV stopped, he jumped out and ran to the front door where he was greeted by his mother. "Mom, I've missed you so much!"

They wrapped each other in a mutual hug, tears choking her words. "Thank God you're safe."

When she half released him, Adam bent down to embrace his father who sat in his wheelchair. "Dad, I'm so sorry."

Ansen patted his grown son with hearty taps on the back. "I'm alive and making progress every day. I've worried about you far more than myself."

Looking up, he saw Ensley, who had pushed Ansen's chair. She practically fell into his arms and he held her, not knowing what to say, and not caring. Simple words finally came. "I've missed you."

The corners of her eyes were damp and she wiped them dry as she sniffed. "I've missed you, too."

Bree shooed them toward the dining room. "A feast awaits our too-long-gone son. I hope you're all hungry."

When Adam spied the table, he saw the comfort foods of his youth. "Pot roast, potatoes with veggies, hot buttered rolls. I'm not hungry, I'm starved."

She beamed with apparent pride. "I hoped that you would like it." Now blushing, she gave a happy order. "Take a seat and dig in as we rejoice in your return."

Everyone ate as each gave snippets of updates on what had transpired in the two months since their last dinner together. Adam purposely gave a glossy overview of his seeming return from the dead, not wanting to frighten his parents. "I passed out and came to just in the nick of time."

Ansen gave an update of his daily grind of therapy, noting his ever-so-slow, but very real progress. "I can swing one foot in front of the other on my own on the parallel bars."

Adam felt relived. "That's the best news I've heard in a long time. You're an inspiration."

Sharing credit, Ansen praised Bree. "Your mother has been right there every step of the way. As I've done with the council, she's temporarily stepped away from Third Rock Sustainability to wheel me around and cheer me up when I'm at the end of my rope. I'm getting my money's worth from that 'in sickness and in health' marriage vow."

Adam and Ens laughed at Ansen's humor while Bree blushed. "It's the least I can do after all the times you risked your life for me."

Seeing his mother on the verge of crying, Adam turned the conversation. "Ens, how are you holding up with two full-time jobs?"

It seemed to Adam that her black hair shimmered more than usual in the dining room lighting as she answered. "It's easier than you might imagine. Because of what you're doing in Venezuela, the Twenty-Three Chromosomes Foundation and Tree of Life Society agendas have a remarkable degree of overlap. Both are figuring out exactly how, or if they are going to be involved."

He took in a deep breath. "Yeah. That's part of the reason I came back to the States for a few days. Troops are massing on the Brazilian side of the border and we're not sure when, or if they will invade. From what we can tell, there is division between the WAGE people and the commanders on the ground. It's tense right now and I know this isn't Society business, strictly speaking, but I could use some allies."

Ens spoke for both organizations. "In the ideal world what would you want from each?"

Adam ran his hand through his shaggy brown hair, which hadn't seen a barber in over two months. "Ideally, a spare army to join us, but since that's not a real possibility, a public statement from a high official in another country supporting us would help. Lockland Woolums is a society member and is the Australian Secretary of Defense. What are the odds he could be persuaded to put out a press release supporting what we're doing? It might make some other nations at least think twice before adding more troops to a volatile situation."

Ansen sat straighter in his wheelchair as he answered. "We go back a long way. Your mother and I met him as teens training in China with Master Lee. I think we could make that happen. There are several other officials at cabinet levels around the world who may also be able to lend their voice to the cause, even if not able to send troops. What else do you need?"

That answer helped, but it was only one brick in a big wall he needed to build. "We could also use some financial pressure on countries that have already committed troops, especially Brazil. My bank has done that, but the Society's financial resources trump mine by several factors."

Ensley wore a Mona Lisa smile, leaving Adam guessing. "That's tricky. Society members and businesses are already pouring money into Venezuela as investments, and to support you. I'm sure we can leverage some pressure on other countries, but there is a fiduciary responsibility not to harm individual members or cause a loss for the Society. Besides, this is a world-wide event, and even the Society's resources are dwarfed by what's going on. Still, I'll see what I can come up with." She smiled again, then asked a follow-up question. "And how can the foundation help?"

With her face returning to that ambiguous smile, the thought crossed his mind that she looked angelic tonight, and he liked it. "That's simple. Come out with a statement extending endorsement for support of Anywhere Solutions soldiers, just as you do for us GM people."

His request turned her smile flat. "That's not as easy. The board has been split on that, and I don't see a consensus coming soon. And to be frank, after what happened to Maddy with that boyfriend of hers, I'm not exactly leaning that way."

That hurt, but he understood. "Listen, I get it. Rex was an A-number-one asshole and got what he deserved. What I've learned being around those guys is that they're like everyone else I've met. Some are great, some terrible, and most somewhere in between."

"I guess I'll have to take your word on that."

She didn't sound convinced, so he pitched a new idea. "Listen, Maddy is coming as the headliner for the Freedom for All festival next weekend. Why not join her, and you can meet some of the guys and get a better sample of what they're like."

She seemed to light up at the idea. "And we could all hang out together for a while. I think I can make that happen."

Adam felt relived and happy. "That's what I was hoping you would say."

The conversation shifted back to catching up with each other mode, and stayed light for the next two hours. Then Adam asked Ens if she would like to share a ride back to the city, which she promptly accepted. Goodbyes were said by all and the two of them loaded into a black SUV for the ride.

Bree and Ansen watched as they pulled away in the dark night until the taillights were out of sight. She looked down at her husband. "They're really adults now, aren't they?"

She could see him stiffen as he answered. "Adam's trying to stabilize a nation and Ensley's running two global organizations at the same time. I would definitely call that adulting."

She spoke wistfully as she put a hand on her husband's shoulder. "I hope they can find their way back to each other. Life is hard enough with a committed partner sharing the load, it must seem the weight of the world bearing it alone."

Ansen put a hand over hers. "We're lucky to have each other. Let's hope the same can happen for them."

CHAPTER FORTY-THREE

Ensley woke resting comfortably in Adam's embrace. While two months ago her heart was on fire with the thought that it might be the last time she would see him, last night's lovemaking felt more like the coming back together of two eternally linked souls. That equally comforted and scared the hell out of her. *How am I going to tell him? What will he say?* She wrapped his right hand between hers when he stirred. "Good morning."

He pulled her close, like two spoons in the silverware drawer. "Any morning with you is a good morning."

The bitterness of their divorce felt a thousand miles away as she surrendered to his muscular embrace. Words rising from her core were whispered in the early morning light. "I've missed you."

"And I've missed you, too. I could hold you like this all day and be happy."

With her face warming, she turned to look at him, her smile sincere. A lock of his uncut hair hung down in a slack curl, and she pushed it back, her finger gliding over his tan skin. "Let's turn our phones off and have an 'us' day. Just you and me, with no outside distractions."

Leaning close, his kiss was gentle. "That's an idea I can get behind."

She moved closer, her kisses more assertive as she pushed him back, rolling on top. Their synchronized movements requiring no thought, only reaction based on their familiarity with each other's wants and needs. His hands touched places that made her moan and her lips landed with greetings of ooh's and ah's. They ended on their backs, looking up at the ceiling, like so many times in the preceding years. She wanted the moment to last forever, but a stomach growl as loud as a tiger's roar caused her to laugh, breaking the spell. "Shower, then breakfast?"

"I'll wash your back if you'll wash mine."

After a bubbly, playful shower, he manned the stove wearing only a tee-shirt and boxers. As he had so many times before when they were married, he made fluffy omelets stuffed with spinach, grated cheddar, and cherry tomatoes, all seasoned with salt and pepper. He slid her plate across the broad kitchen island. "Just like the old days."

The aroma of the familiar spices and ingredients further triggered her nostalgia of their happiest days. Taking the first bites only added to the sensation of being sucked into a time warp, taking her mind back to those best times. *I wish it were possible to go back to those simpler days, but life is more complicated now.* She closed her eyes and for a moment put those thoughts aside, instead savoring the meal. "A taste of heaven."

Sitting beside her, he wolfed down half of his breakfast before slowing to enjoy sips of strong coffee. "This was always your favorite combination. Seemed like a good way to start the day..." He teased. "Or should I say continue the day."

The rest of their breakfast was leisurely, punctuated by the sharing of random memories, like the time they were snowed in for three days at a ski cabin outside of Aspen. They subsisted only on beer, saltine crackers and beef jerky. She complemented his ingenuity. "I still can't believe you made a casserole one night."

He chuckled. "And the leftovers weren't too bad for breakfast the next morning."

With their meal finished and dirty dishes placed in the washer, she wanted nothing more than to lounge away the day recalling other memories from their past. But there was something she needed to tell him, and putting it off wouldn't make the discussion any easier. She had been trying to think of a way to ease into the subject, but hadn't come up with anything, so she decided to wing it. "What are your plans after this crisis in Venezuela is over?"

He ambled to a cushy leather chair in her living room, pulling her down on his lap, her sheer white nightgown matching hit tee-shirt. "I've been going ninety miles per hour getting the country running, and haven't given it much thought." He paused for a few seconds. "I guess more of the same. It's taken a couple of decades of mismanagement to create the current mess, and six months of hard work won't fix it." He pushed her damp hair behind her ear. "How about you? What are your plans?"

She was determined to keep her composure, answering truthfully. "I'm sure I'll be busy, too."

Adam nodded. "Running two global organizations must be a juggling nightmare, with an ever-increasing number of balls in the air." His eyes brightened. "But by then, maybe my father will be recovered enough to resume his role as patriarch."

That thought genuinely touched her heart. "Let's hope so, he's working so hard on his recovery." She looked into his blue eyes. "But I'll be busy by then with a new challenge. One I'm going to love, even though it scares me to death."

She could see the confusion on his face. "What's going on? Are you taking on another job?"

Shifting her shoulders side to side she, answered. "Kind of, but the pay is lousy. I do hear that it's the best job I'll ever have."

"I'm not that good at riddles so..." He stopped mid-sentence, his eyes widening and his voice tightening. "Are you saying what I think you're saying?"

Her eyes blinked twice. "I think you're better at riddles than you give yourself credit." Her Mona Lisa smile of the evening before returned, not sure of the reaction she might get to her next words. "I'm pregnant."

Adam didn't blink as he met her gaze, then he swallowed hard, before answering with a single word. "Wow."

The edges of her lips crept up as he hadn't reacted negatively. "I kind of felt the same way when I found out."

With a quiver in his voice, he said words that she couldn't tell if were spoken as a question, or a statement. "Then *we're* having a baby..."

Her head nodded as she struggled to hold it together, fearful that anything she might say could tilt the situation in an unwelcome direction.

He pulled her close, then kissed the top of her head. "I once hoped this day might happen, but I had kind of given up on the idea...you know? I mean with all that's happened between us."

She couldn't tell if he was happy, or just stunned. "What are you thinking?"

He hugged her in a long silent embrace. "Truthfully, I'm shocked. I mean I *think* I kind of like the idea, but why didn't you tell me this is what you wanted?"

Ensley kept her head buried in his hug. "You were going to war... and I thought I might lose you. I thought back on our lost time and just..." She tried to make verbal sense of what her gut had driven her to do. "Things seemed to be starting to maybe click between us again, and I had been daydreaming about what life would be like if we did get back together, and it definitely included children...so I just decided it was something I had to try." Guilt about making this choice without telling him spilled out. "I figured I probably wouldn't get pregnant anyway, so I decided to keep quiet."

"But you did."

Her cheeks reddened as she confessed. "It was selfish, bordering on unethical not to tell you." She looked back up seeing a stunned expression. "I hope you don't hate me."

He held her in silence, and when he did speak, he sounded in a daze. "My life is so crazy right now. I don't know how I'm going to make this work."

Hearing him contemplate a future, even if it was complicated, gave her hope. "We have a few months. We can figure it out."

Adam muttered as his head shook. "A baby? You a mother? Me a father?"

"Yep...it's a lot." She waited in his embrace as he processed the news.

Finally, he uttered words that sent her spirit soaring. "It's not the way I would have planned it...but I guess I'm the luckiest man in the world."

She had promised herself she wasn't going to cry, but realized now that it was inevitable, and gave in to the primal urge. Through tears of relief, she replied. "And I'm the happiest woman."

He laughed, which surprised her. "You know, my mom will go bonkers when she finds out. She might challenge you for that 'happiest woman' title."

CHAPTER FORTY-FOUR

Adam had been back in Venezuela for three days and the demands of bringing the country back to life after decades of mismanagement was just as unrelenting as when he left. In addition, reports of reinforcements arriving for the growing potential invasion force on the other side of the border increased the tension for everyone. The main reason for his nonstop smile was learning that he was going to be a father in a few months, and that Ensley and Maddy were flying down together tomorrow. That was the first topic in his meeting with President Alverez. "People are already lining up to get into the show. It's a huge boost to national morale."

The president questioned. "Do you think it's a good idea to be celebrating when we could be at war any day?"

"Alejandro, our intelligence shows the opposition forces growing, but we don't have any indication that an invasion is imminent." He glanced out the restored palace windows, seeing workers in white overalls patching and painting the bullet riddled capitol building. "You and I have pushed so hard and so fast that the citizens need an outlet. A Madeline Blaze concert broadcasted live to the nation will generate a tremendous amount of good will. Good will we'll sorely need if we have to soon ask for their support against foreign forces."

Looking presidential in his crisp, starched white shirt and razor-sharp pressed slacks, Alejandro began to pace. "You are right about the good will, but I don't share your assessment of the timing of a potential invasion. I know Santos, and he is as crazy and unpredictable as they come. He could wake up in the morning and say he was told by angels in a dream to invade immediately, and his army would advance, whether they were ready or not."

Hearing the surname of the Brazilian president momentarily soured Adam's mood. "Paulo Santos is a madman, but you think he's that crazy?"

"Oh, I know so. Three years ago, he devalued the Brazilian Real because of a tarot card reading. It threw their economy into a tailspin for months, but he never apologized. He said he had prevented an even greater disaster, though he never spelled out exactly what that meant."

Adam drummed his fingers on the gold inlaid table, thinking of options. He desperately wanted to see Ensley and Maddy, but didn't want to put them in danger. He threw out an idea. "Duce tells me that we've got about a third of our fighter jets back in service. Let's double the flights along the border, just to remind the troops on the other side that even if they were to mount a successful invasion, it's going to be a bloody fight."

Alejandro's hands went out and shoulders shrugged. "It makes sense for the sane commanders on the ground, but we're back to the original problem. Santos' mind makes decisions according to its own rules, without regard to reality. Who knows what he will do?"

Adam stood and joined the president, staring out at the capitol under reconstruction. He crossed his arms, clad in his now ubiquitous army uniform. "We can't live paralyzed lives, awaiting the whims of a crazed man. I say we move forward, living to the fullest, not cowering in the face of bullies. We prepare for both peace and war, hoping for the former but ready for the latter."

Extending a hand to Adam's shoulder, Alejandro reminded him of recent history. "You are in charge of the military, so I'll defer to your decision. Just remember, two months ago President Rojas thought he had all the angles covered...until Volkov invaded and took the country. History shows us we shouldn't discount crazy men."

CHAPTER FORTY-FIVE

Adam waited on the airport tarmac as Maddy's plane touched down at the Simón Bolívar International Airport. He had spoken to Ensley last night as she was about to meet Maddy and join her on the flight. She seemed giddy at the prospect of sharing the good news of her pregnancy with her best friend, and enjoying a few days of all three together. Adam just hoped Maddy wouldn't slip up and say something about their tryst. *That could really change the whole mood of this trip.*

The plane came to a full stop and a set of stairs were rolled plane side. The door opened and a thought raced. *I'll know soon enough if Maddy kept our rendezvous just between us.*

Maddy appeared at the top of the stairs first and gave a wave to Adam. *So far, so good.* Ensley was close behind as Maddy took her first steps down. His heart raced just seeing Ens, and his hand sprung up, waving to her.

Her reaction to seeing him was to look down, avoiding eye contact. His hand came down like a kite falling when the wind stopped blowing. *This can't be good.* Trying to guess what had transpired in the prior few hours, it seemed obvious that Maddy had told Ensley about what had happened. He tried to justify his actions to himself. *But Ens and I weren't even back together...and Maddy came on to me, not the other way around.*

Maddy took the final step and landed on Venezuelan soil. She leaned in and whispered. "We need to talk."

What the hell is going on? His brain was on fire, mad at himself and at Maddy, but he kept his cool outwardly. "Uh, sure. But I need to welcome Ensley first."

Her answer unsettled him even more. "I'll wait for you in the front car. She'll be riding separately."

He greeted Ens as she took the final step off of the portable stairs. "I'm so happy you're here."

Looking up, bloodshot eyes stared as if to injure him, her words ice-cold. "We'll talk later." With that, she headed to the second car in the convoy that would take them, as well as Maddy's band and crew into the city.

This is bad. Turning, he joined Maddy in the lead vehicle. Settling in and closing the door, he faced her. "What did you tell her?"

Pulling away, the line of SUV's began the long drive into the city. "I owe you an explanation."

"You think?" His exasperation dripped. "We enjoyed a couple of days together, and I stress the word enjoyed, but we agreed it was nothing more, right?"

"Yes...but things changed."

"Apparently." Adam answered acerbically. "Why would you tell her? Surely she told you her good news, and you still felt you had to share what happened between us?" His emotions bubbled. "Besides, it was you that pushed that night, not me." He immediately regretted his words. "Sorry. That came out all wrong. I didn't exactly put up the biggest fight, not at all. The truth is I wanted those couple of days as much as you."

Maddy rested her hand on his. "Life is unpredictable."

Distraught over how this reunion with Ens was playing out, he snapped. "Life is unpredictable? That's what you're going with?"

"Chill for a minute, and you'll see what I mean."

His lips pursed as he worked to reign in his emotions. "This better be good."

"Believe me, it will be cray-cray." She squeezed his hand, took in a deep breath, and began. "Life with Rex was like living on a rollercoaster. Looking back, I know now how unstable it was, but when you're in the middle of the ride it's hard to see the big picture."

"Unstable? He tried to kill you."

"You don't have to remind me. I went to therapy, remember?" She paused as she looked up for a moment. "But in our up and down world, terrible moments were almost always spaced between unbelievable highs. When things were good, they were incredible. So incredible that we planned a wonderful future... including a family."

Adam shot back, immediately catching her inference. "You're pregnant...with his child?"

With lowered eyes, Maddy answered slyly, her voice rising. "Would you believe you're half right?"

Adam's head slowly turned toward her, picking up on the implication of her words. *Damn it!* He spoke incredulously. "You've got to be kidding...those two days?"

Maddy seemed fully in control of her emotions, speaking calmly. "Uh, huh. Talking with my doctor, I'm almost positive that's the case. Those Anywhere Solutions men have animal genes spliced into their genome, and it isn't easy for them to get a woman knocked up. Rex and I had already started looking into invitro, and I was on fertility drugs. We'll definitely test the baby when it's born, but doing the math based on my due date, I'm pretty sure you're the baby daddy."

Head spinning, he tried to choose his words carefully, remembering the first time he had screwed up this kind of delicate conversation with Kimee, and not wanting to make the same mistakes again. "I take it from Ensley's reaction, she knows?"

The confirming nod was slow and certain. "Yep." She squeezed his hand again. "As I was saying, life is unpredictable."

Adam stared blankly, stunned. After a short silence, he turned toward her. "My head is spinning like a top, but you've had some time. What do you think about all this?"

"My mind is blown."

"I get that." He tried not to let sarcasm rule his thoughts. While dazed, he and Maddy had known each other forever, and he tried to react as a friend, but instead blurted out his real feelings. "Both of you ended up pregnant, and neither mentioned your intentions to me. That would have been nice, you know?"

Maddy looked straight ahead, waiting to reply. "That's fair. The question now is, whatcha wanna do?"

Adam rubbed his temples as if having a migraine, hoping to at least help himself focus on the right words to say. "This situation is insane. Not one, but two babies on the way, with two different women." He pushed the heels of his palms into his eyes. "And not just any two women. You and Ens mean more to me than anyone else in the world." His hands dropped to his lap and his eyes followed. "It's a lot to process."

"It's wacko, right?"

He turned toward her. "And what do you think about you and me having a baby?"

Maddy smiled. "Rex and I had been talking about having a little one, so I had already started to think about having a little Joey in the pouch. But I didn't anticipate it happening like this, with you that weekend. I promise. But as reality has set in, I'm excited, very excited. I think we'll have the cutest little chunk." She shook her head. "Then I think about you, me, and Ens..."

His head shook as well. "Imagine pitching a movie plot where a guy's ex-wife and his oldest friend are both expecting at the same time. It would have to be some kind of Romcom." His mind turned to Ensley. "Or maybe it would be a murder mystery. When you two arrived, she gave me a look that could kill. What happened on that plane?"

Maddy had been calm talking about her own pregnancy, but being asked about her conversation with Ens seemed to shake her. "It was super awk, for real. I mean, I didn't know you two had gotten close again, I swear, and you didn't mention it either. I mean, a couple months ago you two were barely on speaking terms."

"We hadn't got back together then, I promise." He closed his eyes tight, then opened them as he looked out the window. "That happened the day I went back to New York." He laughed at his predicament. "I've always had great timing." His thoughts raced until the car hit a bump, jarring him back to their unfinished discussion. "How did your little chat with Ens go down?"

"When we met to fly down here, I was so happy. I kind of just blurted out, 'I'm pregnant!'"

He rubbed his forehead. "And she responded, how?"

"She was just as thrilled, so we hugged and she made her announcement. 'I'm pregnant, too!' Then she added the kicker. 'Adam and I are so excited.'"

"Sorry. It feels awkward just to hear you describe it." He pressed. "But you have to tell me the rest."

Maddy's white skin seemed paler. "My face must have looked like I was hit by a chair, because she was all like, 'what's wrong?' We sat down just as the plane took off, giving me a few minutes to get my shit together. We've known each other too long to lie."

This is going to be bad, but I have to know. He spoke, sounding defeated. "What happened next?"

She turned to face Adam. "I told her the truth...about that night at my beach cottage... after I had killed Rex. I told her I made you stay for dinner, that we got drunk and high and that I had come on to you, that it wasn't your idea."

This didn't change the situation, but it was a relief that Maddy had told the story the way he remembered it. "How did she react?"

"She cried...a lot."

Adam's fingers squeezed his forehead like a vice. "It pains me just to hear you tell it." He sighed. "But go on, I have to hear it all."

A slight quiver traced her response. "She asked if we were serious, or if it was a one-weekend hook up. I think she was trying to decide the same about you two, in light of what she had just learned."

"Damn. How did you answer?"

"I told her the truth. You and I have only spoken a few times since then, and never a word about a shared future." Maddy sighed. "I was totally fine with that two months ago. We had some fun, and I wasn't expecting anything else...but I guess we need to have a convo, yeah?"

"Yeah, I guess so." His hand ran through his hair. "I'm assuming I'm the father until proven otherwise, okay?"

"Thank you. That means a lot."

"We're all rich by any definition, but just to say it out loud, I'm totally committed to doing what's right for the child."

Maddy nodded. "We're lucky, compared to so many others." She laughed. "I remember the night when you told your parents about Kimee. They crushed you, and you totally beat yourself up over it."

Adam released a tense breath and laughed himself. "I'm so smart at so many things, but *this* seems to be my Achilles heel. At least I feel like I'm handling finding out I'm going to be a father a little better this time around, but there are way more conventional ways to do this." He laughed again. "Speaking of my mother, she was over the moon when Ens and I told her our news. I'm sure she's going to be stunned, but I know her, and I know she'll be just as excited by this development."

That made Maddy smile. "I hope so. With my mom gone, she's the closest thing to a mother I have."

Feeling a sense of equilibrium returning, Adam held her hand. "I want to be a father to this child in every way I can, even though I don't know exactly how you and I work out the details. Are you good with leaving it there for right now?"

She teased. "I guess I can cut you some slack. I mean, you've had fifteen whole minutes to think about it."

His smile was sincere. "Thanks." Then his mind went to the vehicle behind them and the smile dissolved. "And now I need to have a talk with the woman in the next car. That's going to be weird, because an hour ago I was happy and dreaming about what our future might hold."

"Say, I just remembered something from the old days, back at Chalky's."

Adam's eyes widened. "Crazy stuff happened there. I can't wait to hear this."

Her words seemed to come directly from those long-ago times. "You and Ens had just gotten together, but we had detected a spark between us, and I asked you about it. Do you remember what you said?"

He felt transported back to the moment, flush with the feeling of first love. "Yeah, I do. It was something like, 'this is going to be weird for all of us, but can we make it a little weird instead of a lot weird?"

Maddy nodded. "Exactly. It was good advice ten years ago, and it still is. You and I are friends who had a two-day fling. But you and Ens have real history...like marriage history. I'm not down for hurting Ens any more than has already happened. Don't let this ruin everything between you two, please?"

"From your lips to God's ears, because I think it might take divine intervention to work this out."

She spoke wistfully. "Like I said, life is unpredictable."

CHAPTER FORTY-SIX

Ensley had hoped to get pregnant when Adam went to war with Volkov, knowing he might not survive. Reconnecting with him last week had made her feel like it was one of the best decisions she had ever made. She had expected a joyful reunion with Adam today, right up until she got on the plane to travel with Maddy to Venezuela. The conversation they had cast doubt on the wisdom of everything from the past two months. Her mind tumbled the same thought over and over as her SUV trailed theirs to the J W Marriott hotel in downtown Caracas. *He's the same philandering man he's always been.*

Adam had made all the arrangements, so she bypassed the check-in desk and traveled straight to a suite on the top floor. She collapsed on the bed, fatigued from travel, pregnancy, and the emotional blow of learning of Adam and Maddy's fling. "I just need to sleep."

Waking when her phone rang, she looked at the time. "Wow. Two hours? No way." Seeing the name of the caller, she wearily answered before it went to voicemail. "Adam."

"Hope I'm not bothering you."

She blinked hard a couple of times, trying to fully wake up. "No,

I crashed for a while. I was just getting up." She fibbed and didn't know why.

"If you're hungry, maybe we could have dinner...perhaps talk a little?"

She heard the caution in his voice and answered with sarcasm. "No, Adam. I'm not really feeling a night on the town, if you know what I mean."

There was a long pause on the other end before he answered. "We could order room service and dine on the balcony. The city is beautiful at sundown, and we really do need to talk."

He's right about that, and that at least gives me time to get my mind right. "I guess we could do that. Eight o'clock?"

"I'll see you then."

Time seemed to speed by, and before she knew it, there was a knock on the door. She opened it, seeing Adam, who had changed from the camo uniform he was wearing at the airport into gray slacks and a yellowish-orange hibiscus button down. She was mad as hell at him, but a thought forced its way into her conscious, *you still look good.* Her words were neutral. "Come in."

He stepped through the double door of the luxury suite. "I hope you like the place. I asked them to put you in the best suite."

She glanced around the spacious living area separated from the decadent bedroom and massive bathroom. She could care less about the suite with her mind on their coming discussion. "It's nice."

Walking toward the sliding door, he stated the obvious. "That mountain view is incredible."

Placing her hand on her stomach, she restructured priorities. "Hey, I'm starved. Let's place our order before I eat everything in the mini-bar."

His grin made boyish dimples in his cheeks, and her earlier

anger toward him ebbed a half notch as he answered. "I'm ready to eat, and I'm grabbing a beer from the fridge as well. Want one?"

Her head fell as she patted her belly, which wasn't showing yet. "You're going to need to get used to water and the occasional soda for me for the next few months."

His cheeks reddened. "Sorry. Yeah, I wasn't thinking."

She was still pissed at him, but chuckled at his embarrassment. "Bring me a candy bar and a bottle of juice, and let's get this order placed."

Doing as told, he stood beside her as they reviewed their dinner options from the room service menu. Just his presence so close felt good, but her feelings were still jangled. *Must be the hormones.* "I'll take the snapper and risotto." She peeled the wrapper to the candy bar and added emphasis. "And tell them to hurry."

He called in the order as she made her way to the huge outdoor area. When he joined, he opened his beer and took a sip, then sat quietly.

I guess he's waiting on me to go first...and that's probably smart. Swallowing a bite of the chocolate appetizer, then washing it down with mango juice, she opened up. "I was stunned, hurt and felt betrayed when Maddy told me she was pregnant...with your baby." Reliving that moment in her mind brought those feelings back anew and her words bit hard. "How could you? How could she? Do you understand why I'm upset?"

Adam took a bigger drink from the sweated bottle. "Yes. I understand why you're upset." He spoke calmly, without a trace of defensiveness. "I think she told you what happened that weekend, and just so you know, I was stunned myself when she told me she was expecting. I am still stunned...just like I was when you told me the same thing a few days ago."

Touché. I guess I deserved that. "I should have told you I was actually trying to get pregnant, that I feared you would be killed. But still, how could you?" There was an emotional hitch in her voice as she continued. "How could she? She's my best friend and you and I were married...once. That's not right."

Draining his beer, he stood. "Hold that thought, I'll be right back." He returned with another bottle, taking a long first drink. "Yes. You should have told me...but that's water under the bridge now, isn't it? Perhaps you'll judge me a little less harshly for some of the rash things I've done in the past. We're not perfect, even if our genes are."

She knew he was right. He should have been part of that decision, but still... "That's true, but you and Maddy? That feels like betrayal on so many levels, and it hurts."

"I won't speak for her, just for myself." He took another gulp. "Just so you know, this is awkward for me as well." Leaning back, he looked toward the mountains, now bathed in the final golden rays of the setting sun. "Since puberty there has been a curiosity about both of you. I mean our lives were...*are* so weird, and you two are the only women in the world who truly understand what we've all been through. In hindsight, it almost seems inevitable."

"But we were married!" The root of the pain was spoken loudly. "Some things are supposed to be off limits!"

Staring at him, she saw a ripple in his jaw as he seemed to quash his emotions while answering calmly. "I agree, so once you and I became a couple, I set any feelings for her aside." His shoulders squared. "And I screwed up when we were married, I did, but there was never a thought to be with her while we were married. Never."

She felt tears welling, but breathed in a few times to give herself space to keep them contained. A gentle breeze blew a lock of hair in her face and she swept it back, ready to continue. "But that weekend?" Her words pleaded. "Why?"

His gaze stayed on the distant hills as she stared at him. "Like I said, I'll not speak for Maddy or her motives, only myself." He turned toward her, his gaze soft. "We were...*are* divorced. I was days away from heading down here to fight a war where none of us knew with certainty I would survive. In fact, I got shot in the head and almost cremated."

Ensley's chin quivered at that image in her mind. "But still... with Maddy?"

"Look, like she told you, it was Maddy who made the first move, but I didn't put up much resistance. Like I said earlier, I had always been curious. You and I had barely spoken for years, and I had no real expectation we would rekindle our romance like we have. I swear on everything I hold precious, there was never an intention to hurt you. Never." He took a deep breath. "That's what happened, and here we are."

Everything he said was true, but the sense of betrayal lingered. "And now? What do you want?" He took another drink of beer, and for a moment she wished she could as well, but her thoughts grounded her. *I have another life to nurture. No alcohol.*

"It's the only thing I've thought about since you two arrived." He tapped the now empty bottle on the table. "What I've realized is that what I want only matters if it's what both of you want."

She pushed her hair behind her ear again, even though it didn't need it. "But if it *was* only up to you? What then?"

The bottle tapped a couple more times. "If I were king of the world..." He gave a dismissive laugh. "That's a joke. My personal life is like a bad movie and an army is massing on the border primed to kill me. I'm just trying to keep everything I hold dear from falling apart at the same time."

She was shocked. "I've really only thought about what's happening to me, from my perspective." Her anger ebbed another notch. "I guess it's been kind of overwhelming for you, too." The sun finally dipped completely below the horizon, leaving them in the twilight between night and day. "Still, I have to know what you want."

He turned completely and took her hands in his, his eyes seeming tender and sincere. "Most of all, I want to be the best father I can to these children being born into this bizarre situation. This predicament is not of their doing, and I don't want them to suffer from our decisions."

Her thoughts traced back to stories she had heard about their own births under even more unusual and dire circumstances. Their parents had risked their lives to have them, and they raised them as best as they could in their own trailblazing way. "I agree. We put the children's needs first. They are the innocents in all of this." His hands squeezed hers, and the familiar feel went straight to her core, like an unbidden bolt of endorphins, triggering warm feelings. *Hold your emotions, you don't know what he's going to say next.*

"I'm far from perfect and I've made a lot of mistakes, but even when I failed, I always loved you." Despite the dim lighting, she could see his eyes glistening. "Maddy will always be a friend like no other in the world, and we'll share the raising of her child..." There was a catch in his voice as he continued. "But Ensley, *you* are the only one I love, and I'll *never* stop loving you."

Even though she was still mad, his words shot straight to her heart like a guided missile. As if on autopilot, she leaned toward him. He matched her movement, their lips meeting in a soft kiss. A loud knock on the door interrupted the moment. A smile forced its way onto her face. "The food's here."

Adam stood, still holding her hands. "I better let them in, you're eating for two, and a candy bar and mango juice aren't enough."

It was the first time anyone had mentioned her pregnancy in

that familiar, yet new to her way. While not bawling, a single tear had rolled down each cheek, so she pulled her hands away to wipe them. "I guess I'm going to have to make a few adjustments to my diet and eating schedule." He headed to the door, leaving her in her thoughts. *Who am I kidding? I'm going to be making a thousand adjustments, especially as Adam, Maddy and me figure all this out.*

CHAPTER FORTY-SEVEN

Adam woke early, fully clothed with Ensley in his arms, his hand draped over her thin waist. After dinner, they had cuddled and she drifted off to sleep. His thoughts turned to the child she was carrying, his child. *I can't wait to meet you, but your mom and I have a lot of things to work out, so let's take our time. Okay?*

The busy day ahead intruded into his thoughts and he prioritized. *I need to get the latest on troop movements along the border, then make sure Maddy's team has everything they need to get set for the concert tonight.*

He moved ever so slightly, and Ens awoke in a start. "What's happening? Where am I?"

"Sorry I woke you. You went out like a light last night and haven't moved."

She stretched and yawned. "What time is it anyway?"

Morning light streamed into the suite as he looked to the bedside clock. "Six-thirty. I hate to leave, but there's a lot going on today."

It felt good to see her smile as she answered. "Go do what you need to do, I'll be fine. I might even text Maddy and see if she wants to join me for breakfast."

He froze. "Oh?"

She playfully poked his chest. "You and I worked out some things last night, and us girls need to do the same." She must have read his face. "Don't worry, we're all going to get through this. After all we are the three amigos, remember?"

Before answering, he leaned in for a kiss. "I think that's what we all want. To find our new normal and be there for each other, just like always."

He started to get out of bed when she grabbed his hand. "Hey. You said something last night and we were interrupted by dinner's arrival before I could answer."

"What? You'll have to refresh my memory."

She sat up, her face serious. "You told me that I was the only one you loved and would never stop loving me."

He could feel his cheeks warm. "Yeah, and I meant it. I'm not perfect, but I got that part right."

"This all feels shaky...but deep down I feel the same way." Now her cheeks blushed like a red rose. "We've got a ways to go, but I would still like to give us another try."

They embraced and he wanted nothing more than to spend the day here with her, but he knew that wasn't possible. "I don't want to leave, but I have to. I'll call, then swing by and pick you up before Maddy's show." He leaned in for another kiss, then said words he had said a thousand times, but rarely felt as sweet as today. "I love you."

"I love you, too."

He stood and walked out of the room backwards, keeping her in sight as long as he could. His security detail was downstairs and as soon as he stepped outside the hotel, he was back in the dangerous world that was his life. "Take me to HQ. I need a change of clothes, then we try to save our little slice of heaven."

Within an hour, his morning embrace of Ens seemed like an alternate timeline, one where war was not a real possibility. Duce was providing an update on the latest troop movement info. "Our warning flights along the border seem to have had no effect on activities on the ground. More tanks have been moved into forward positions."

Glancing toward the president, Adam asked about allies. "Anything new on outside help coming our way?"

President Alverez chuckled. "Out of the blue, we got a statement of support from the Australian Secretary of Defense to add to the other words of encouragement we've received from several governments. Like them, he's not offering troops, but it was a nice sentiment."

Well, at least the Society followed through, but it's becoming crystal clear this is above what even they can do. "You don't say. We should at least send a cable indicating our appreciation."

"Already sent." Alejandro looked worried. "We're not getting any outside help, are we? That WAGE group stirred this pot of hate and the crazy man to our south latched onto the myth. We're on our own."

The word WAGE rang in Adam's ears in ways they would never understand. An evil thought wormed its way into his consciousness. *Would today be different if we had killed Becky and Kelley that night in the warehouse?* He shook his head, literally trying to rid himself of negative thoughts. "We can't worry about those people today. We have to focus on the here and now, and that's the force gathered across the border, and our response if they invade."

Z entered the briefing room with news. "Images from our drones show ammunition being loaded into covered vehicles, suggesting an attack sometime within the next three days."

This was not what he was hoping to hear, especially since both Ensley and Maddy were here. *It's starting to feel like this wasn't my smartest idea.* He stood as he reviewed their defensive strategy. "We can't stop them from crossing into our territory with the arsenal we have at our disposal, but we can spill enough blood to make them wonder if it's worth it." He pointed to Z. "What's the latest on the choke points?"

Pointing to the wall-sized map with a laser pointer, Z lit a dozen points. "These are the narrowest mountain passes through which troops or tanks will have to travel to reach the capitol. Each of them now has fortified machine gun nests on both sides of these naturally occurring geographic locations. It will be like shooting fish in a barrel."

Adam nodded. "Duce, update us on the capitol specific defenses."

Standing, Duce pointed to the president. "Thanks to years of resistance to the former regime, local freedom fighters have a lot of experience blockading streets, harassing enemy soldiers, and fire-bombing stationary positions. Because of the good will we've built the past few months with food aid and new jobs, those informal troops have agreed to fight with us. President Alverez deserves credit for building bridges to those elements of society."

"Those are the strengths of our defense." Adam's voice lowered. "But we do have one gaping weakness. Z, walk us through the air superiority situation."

Z returned to a problem they had discussed for weeks, but hadn't solved. "The Anywhere Solutions invasion degraded the Venezuelan Air Force significantly. Most of the planes were destroyed on the ground, but we saw firsthand how even one or two bombers or fighter jets can completely turn the tables of war. We lost more troops to the small number of planes that were able to launch than any fight we got from ground troops. The opposition doesn't have a huge fleet, but they can fly right over our terrestrial defenses and hit us anywhere they want."

Adam stood. "To win, our people must be willing to sustain loss while we make the cost too high for Santos to bear. We must make the blood of their ground troops flow six inches deep."

Alejandro clasped his hands. "Because so much has been accomplished in such a short time, the people have hope, and that is a powerful bond. They will stand with us because we are all truly in this together."

"Speaking of the people, this morning there were already thousands in line for tonight's concert." Adam scanned the war planners in the room. "Do you think we should proceed?"

Z spoke first. "From a military standpoint, it should absolutely be canceled. If the invasion were to begin during the show, everyone in attendance would be sitting ducks. A single strafing run by a fighter jet would kill thousands, and bombs would kill tens of thousands."

Duce added his weight behind Z. "I totally concur. It's too big of a risk."

"But there are bigger things to consider." Alejandro saw things through a different prism. "We have asked our citizens to trust us, to put up with short-term problems in exchange for long-term rewards. The Libertad Para Todos festival is a small reward that will mean so much! Madeline Blaze came here...to recognize what 'we the people' have done. The good will the concert can generate will help sustain us for hard times that are sure to come. I say the show should go on unless we are sure the invasion begins today."

Adam felt torn. After all they had achieved the people deserved a reward, even if it was only music. But was it worth the risk? Could he live with himself if things went south? Unable to decide in the moment. he split the difference. "We wait until four o'clock this afternoon to make the call. The situation should be clearer by then. The last thing we want is to put our people at unnecessary risk." He looked through the window toward the stadium. *Especially the most important people in my life.*

CHAPTER FORTY-EIGHT

Ensley stared at her phone for several minutes, knowing what she needed to do, but dreading it. She mumbled along as she typed the text. "Would you join me for breakfast? We need to talk." She hit the send button before changing her mind. "There. It's done."

The reply came quickly from Maddy. *I'm starved. Give me 30 to get dressed and I'll meet you downstairs.*

Glancing in the bathroom mirror, Ens spoke to herself. "Never in a million years would I have dreamed up this situation. Our bizarre lives just keep getting stranger." With a few dabs of makeup and a comb through her hair, she felt presentable...but not ready.

The smell of bacon greeted her as she stepped through the open double doors of the high-end hotel restaurant, spotting Maddy at a table near a window, scrolling through her phone. Catching her friend's eye, she waved as she headed that way, not knowing how this encounter would go.

Maddy stood and grabbed her in a hug as soon as Ens was close enough, speaking warmly. "We'll figure this out, right?"

Relief swept over Ens at the sincere greeting. "I hope so." Taking her seat, a waiter came and quickly took their order. She looked across the table with a jumble of unfamiliar emotions, unsure how to start the conversation. *Maddy's my oldest friend. Just keep it simple and speak from the heart.* "How are you feeling?"

"You heard my order." She laughed. "This is the first time I've ever asked for extra bacon and hash browns."

A small laugh escaped. "Same for me on the appetite, and I feel like I need a nap every afternoon."

With the ice broken, Maddy broached the subject that brought them together this morning. She reached for Ens' hand. "I promise, it was never my intention to hurt you."

"Adam said the same thing..." She didn't pull away. In her anger yesterday, everything seemed so clear. Adam and Maddy had crossed a line, and she was the aggrieved party. But now she understood that it was more complicated, even if it hurt. Still, she needed to know more. "Why? What were you thinking?"

"I can tell you a bunch of factors came into play, but it boils down to bad decision making in an unstable state of mind. That, and I had no idea you and Adam were close to hooking back up. I swear on my mother's soul."

"Yeah." Ensley lowered her head. "That happened kind of fast. From what I've learned, it was right after he and you ...well, you know."

"And after what happened with Rex."

While she had talked with Maddy over the phone since then, it dawned on her that this trip was their first time together since that horrific incident. She turned the tables and squeezed her friend's hand. "That must have been truly awful."

Sounding robotic, as if she had said the words over and over and was now numb to their meaning, Maddy replied. "He had it coming."

"That's what I heard." She squeezed again. "God, I'm so thankful you survived."

"Yeah, me too. But that was the triggering event for bring me here this morning. Adam came when I called, and I was an emotional wreck. Mix in a little booze and weed, and voila, a knocked-up singer with an already checkered past. The tabloids are going to eat this up. The real story is so juicy they won't even have to make shit up, like they usually do."

Hearing it laid out so bluntly from her friend's point of view was disturbing but helpful. "That's your truth, but someone else was a willing participant."

Maddy shook her head. "He really did tell me it would be a bad idea, but I didn't listen."

"He could have said no. Just walked away." Ensley's hurt was near the surface. "That's what a real friend would have done."

A devilish smile graced Maddy's face. "I may not know how to pick a good man, but trust me, I damn sure know how to seduce one. He's not one-hundred percent innocent, but he at least tried to do the right thing."

"Still..."

The waiter returned with their breakfast. Maddy put her napkin in her lap. "I've got some questions for you too, but let's eat first." It didn't take long for them both to finish their plates, so Maddy restarted their conversation. "We all know how I got this way." She patted her stomach which was unperceptively enlarged. "How did you end up preggers?"

With her belly full, Ens answered impishly. "In the usual way."

"Come on. I've tattled on myself, now you do the same."

Ens pursed her lips while thinking, unsure where to start the tale. "Hmm. I guess it all started the night we all went to Memory Lane. After you and Rex left, Adam apologized again for his philandering and sounded the sincerest I'd heard." She took in a cleansing breath. "I guess I let in a little ray of hope that some-day we might get back together."

Maddy's eyes widened. "And you're in the sack together in what, two weeks? You are the least impulsive person I know, so you've got some explaining to do."

Rubbing the back of her neck, Ens agreed. "Yeah, I've never done *anything* like this, ever." She felt her cheeks warming. "You can at least explain your actions as a response to a traumatic event." The very thought of recalling what she had done caused her to pause. "I *still* have a hard time rationalizing what I did."

"Well, spill your guts, girl. Inquiring minds want to know."

Her chin dipped as she began. "That war stuff started and I couldn't help thinking he might be killed." Looking up, she spoke softly, as if saying it quietly made her story less manipulative. "That sounds stupid, knowing what we do about our genetically enhanced abilities, but I couldn't keep the dark thoughts away. It gnawed and gnawed until I stopped my birth control. I really didn't think I would get pregnant." She mimicked Maddy from a few minutes before by patting her stomach. "But here I am with a bun in the oven, as they say."

Maddy laughed. "At least you weren't on fertility drugs like I was. Rex and I had been trying..."

Arched eyebrows met that comment. "Wow. Did you want to get pregnant with Adam?"

"No! It was just a hookup that I had thought about more than a few times over the years. Since you guys weren't a thing anymore, and I wanted to block out what happened with Rex, I went for it. Like I said, I would never have done it if I knew you wanted to get back together with him."

Ensley reached for Maddy's hand again. "I'm glad we've had this talk. I can't say this isn't weird and uncomfortable, but we'll get through this together...and I do believe you."

Tension seemed to release from Maddy as her shoulders lowered. "Thank you. That will certainly make things easier when we start raising these babies. This isn't a normal situation, but I want to raise this child in the best way I can."

Nodding, Ensley concurred. "I agree, and Adam has said the same thing."

"Speaking of Adam, I know he's not a choir boy, but I hope you two can get past this...this thing with the three of us."

"Yesterday I wasn't sure that would be possible, but we're going to give it a shot."

"That makes me very happy."

She looked directly into Maddy's green eyes. "The three amigos till the end?"

Maddy's face lit with her world-famous smile. "Amigos until the end!"

CHAPTER FORTY-NINE

Becky had been glued to the television for days watching the reporting from South America, getting more upset by the hour. She called to Kelley in the kitchen. "They're saying war is imminent, that tens, maybe even hundreds of thousands will die."

Dark circles around Kelley's blue eyes stood in stark contrast to her pale skin. She joined her wife on the couch. "I've been worried about this. Are you really going to do it? Put all our lives in jeopardy?"

Rocking back and forth as she gnawed on nails already down to the quick, Becky replied. "You know I don't want to, especially because of what might happen to Benz. But Kelley, I've done bad things, things I'll never be able to atone for, and they haunt me to this day. I'll never be able to live with myself if that many innocents die, knowing that I might have been able to stop it."

The CBN reporter on the Brazilian side of the border was talking with a line of tanks as his backdrop. "Reports are that President Santos is prepared to cross the border soon. Working with WAGE, he has assembled a force with contingents from seven other countries. It is a formidable army."

Becky pointed to the television. "That's exactly what I'm talking about. You and I started WAGE and a share of the death that is sure to come is on us. I have to try."

Now Kelley chewed on her nails. "What does Elna say? Is she willing to risk having her daughter outed as modified?"

Staring at the television, Becky didn't answer for a few seconds. "She wasn't crazy about the idea. Plus, she's concerned about the certain ire of her mother. This could destroy her family even if no one learns of Precious' modifications."

"So, she's okay with your plan?"

Another silence followed until Becky spoke in an ominous tone. "Let's just say I persuaded her to see things my way."

"You bullied her, didn't you! I thought you had put that kind of behavior in the rearview mirror."

Becky's rocking continued. "Like it or not, sometimes a woman has to use every tool in her kit."

Kelley put her arm around her wife, stopping the back-and-forth movement. "I understand why you feel you need to do this...and I support you...but it scares the hell out of me."

The reporter gave an update. "Sources say the invasion could come as soon as tonight."

Becky balled her hands into fists. "That's it. I have to do this now...or live with the guilt."

Kelley held her, not saying a word.

A couple of minutes passed as Becky ruminated. *How can I risk my family? How can I not try? Benz's future is too important. Is one life worth more than thousands?* After arguing with herself in her head, she stood, pronouncing judgment. "I'm calling Lesedi, now."

Kelley joined her in standing. "Then I'll call Elna to warn her. Lesedi isn't going to take this well."

Pacing the length of the living room a couple of times mumbling words she planned to use, Becky finally stopped and pulled her phone from her pocket. She spoke to herself as she placed the call. "I have to do this, I *have* to."

On the third ring, Lesedi's distinctive voice called out. "Becky Brown. What a pleasant surprise."

"Yeah." Becky began pacing again. "It's been a while."

"Yes, it has. To what do I owe the pleasure?"

Taking in a steadying breath, Becky prepared to say words she could never take back. *Here goes.* "I'm calling about the imminent war in Venezuela."

Lesedi's reply stiffened. "A difficult, but necessary step to stop the spread of those who would change what it means to be human."

With the phone in her left hand, Becky ran a nervous right hand through her short gray hair. "Look, I don't see it that way. What I know is thousands upon thousands of innocent Venezuelans will be killed in a military operation fomented by a private organization. An organization that I founded. It's immoral and possibly criminal. You have to stop it, or at least try."

"I don't know what happened to you, Becky. You were so committed and such an inspiration that you attracted millions to the cause, but you walked away ten years ago. Now *I'm* in charge. This invasion goes forward."

I didn't want to do this, but you leave me no choice. "Lesedi, sometimes life throws you curveballs you don't expect. They can change your entire perspective on even your deepest beliefs. That's what happened to me...and I'm going to rock your world unless you call off this disaster."

The temper Becky remembered, seemed to reach across the distance between them. "You dare threaten me! You've been away a long time. WAGE now has ways to strike back at our enemies you never dreamed possible, you'll see. I'm going to make your life a living hell!"

While not spiritual, Becky suddenly felt her father's spirit in the room. She heard firm words from the beyond. *No one threatens a Brown and gets away with it.* Nodding silently, Becky's resolve hardened and her tone threatened. "Perhaps you've forgotten who *you're* dealing with. I'm going to tell you two secrets, then listen to you grovel."

"You crazy bitch. I don't have time for this, I'm hanging up."

"Benz is genetically modified." *Let's see if she hangs up now.*

In the silent seconds that followed, Becky could almost hear Lesedi's mind turning over that revelation. An almost maniacal laugh preceded her reply. "I said you were crazy. I should have said insane!" There was another delirious laugh. "I'll destroy you, and Kelley and that subhuman child of yours. Life as you know it is over!"

"Just so you know, Kelley and I didn't plan for Benz to be modified, but it happened."

Lesedi sounded in full rage mode. "I don't give a flying fuck about the how's and why's of your sad life. You...are...doomed!"

The angrier Lesedi became, the calmer Becky felt, knowing that it would make the irate woman's fall more devastating. "Life is funny. We were stunned when we brought him home from the hospital, then amazed as we came to love such an incredible boy. His *precious* life changed everything."

She had dropped the word precious, just to gauge Lesedi's awareness. It seemed to have gone unnoticed. "Insane, sad, misguided..." Sounding arrogant and condescending, Lesedi delivered final condemnation. "You're a pathetic excuse for a human being, and I'm going to enjoy ruining your life."

The Good Book says 'Pride goeth before destruction, and a haughty spirit before a fall.' Here comes the crash. "I said I have two secrets, and you've only heard one. When I finish, you will call off the invasion and never tell anyone about Benz."

Again, there was a momentary silence between them. When Lesedi spoke again, she sounded a little less sure of herself. "I don't believe you...you're bluffing."

"This is your final warning, your last chance to preserve the world as you know it."

Lesedi lashed out. "I'm too busy for this bullshit. Enough with your idle threats."

Sorry, Elna. This must be done. "When women who long to conceive have problems, they become desperate. They're willing to do almost anything to have a child." She paused purposely, to build the stress on the woman on the other end of the call. "Do you know any women who were desperate to have a child? Maybe even in your own family?"

The catch in Lesedi's voice told Becky that her message was delivered and heard. "No. It can't be." She whimpered. "Elna would never do that. Never."

"Desperate people do desperate things. And look at the gift you've received. Precious is such a special young woman." The sympathy and understanding of those words were now replaced with cold callousness. "If you think a public outing of Benz would be a big deal, just think of the teams of international news media that would be camped out in front of your home when I share that secret with the world."

Denial and doubt answered. "No. It can't be. Precious is too perfect."

Becky shot back. "Isn't that the purpose of genetic modification?"

The silence on the other end was deafening, so Becky defined the terms of surrender. "You have one hour to retract your support of the invasion, or your world crumbles. I believe you are smart enough to make the right choice." Becky thought she heard a moan and decided everything that needed to be said, had been said. She reiterated for clarity. "One hour. We'll be watching CBN to hear the unexpected news of your change of heart."

Becky disconnected without waiting for a reply and her thoughts again drifted to her long-gone father. *Ben Brown might not be proud of what I did, but I'm sure as hell he loved how I did it.*

CHAPTER FIFTY

Adam was shocked to see the crawl across the bottom of the television tuned to CBN. "Look at that." He pointed to the screen. "WAGE has pulled their support for an invasion." He shook his head. "Finally, someone must have talked some sense into them."

The president turned to see the message. "That's *wonderful* news."

Hearing the sarcasm, Adam questioned. "It *is* good news. What's your problem, Alejandro?"

The tall, lean man put his hands on his hips. "My problem is I know Santos. He's a megalomaniac and makes his decisions on hunches, feelings and dreams. I don't disagree that having WAGE off our back is a good thing, I just don't think it changes the odds of an invasion."

Adam's shoulders sagged. "Damn. I wish I had a good read on this situation. We're at decision time, and I still don't know what to do about the concert tonight." He turned to Duce and Z. "What's the latest from the border?"

Z offered his assessment. "Images from our drones and fighter flights along the border are inconclusive. They could launch the invasion in a few hours or hang out there for days."

Duce added more info without making the decision any clearer. "Radio chatter has picked up, but most of it is regular soldiers talking about watching our broadcast of the show. Madeline Blaze is a star everyone wants to see."

"That's the root of the problem. I've promised this to our people as a celebration of all we have achieved, and a signal of what we can yet achieve. If we cancel and there is no invasion, there will be a public disappointment cost."

The president gestured with an extended hand toward Adam. "These are your friends. I'll support your decision, but ultimately, this is your call."

Glancing at the time on his cellphone, Adam sighed. "It's five o'clock, an hour past my own deadline. I should have already made this decision." He tapped his foot a few times. "Eighty thousand are already jammed into the stadium hours before the concert, and hundreds of thousands more will be joining in street parties around the country." He stared out the window at the peaceful city. *I hope I don't screw this up.* He spoke words with determination, carrying a whiff of nervousness. "Let's have a party, and hope for the best."

Five hours later, Adam was standing back stage as the local warm-up band was wrapping up. They had done their job getting the audience on their feet and in a good mood. He turned to Maddy, who was going through her pre-concert ritual. "Are you ready?"

Her eyes were closed. "Almost. I'm visualizing a screaming crowd, and looking for the ghost of my mother in the front row. I know it sounds weird, but she was my biggest fan, and I always put on a better show when I sing likes she's here."

Ensley held Adam's hand. "I don't think that's weird at all, Maddy. In fact, I think it's sweet."

With a loud clap of her hands, she broke her own spell. "I'm ready to rock!"

Smiling, Adam reviewed the sequence of events. "After your first number, call me onstage and I'll say a few words thanking you for celebrating with the nation. Then I'll present you as the first recipient of the National Medal of Performing Arts."

She looked touched. "I've won Grammys and dozens of other awards, but this will be one of the most special. Thank you."

"You deserve it." Adam then turned, pointing behind the stage while giving a warning. "Just remember, if something goes sideways, we're getting into that armored troop carrier. It can provide protection while getting us the hell out of here if we need a quick exit."

Waving him off, she declared her mood. "Don't worry so much. It's time to party with Maddy Blaze." With her band in place, the first cords of *Bumps in the Night* began playing. "Wish me luck."

Ens shouted above the music and roaring crowd. "Break a leg!"

Taking a step back, Adam held Ens' hand tight. Bending down he spoke loudly in her ear, trying to be heard above the din. "Sounds like you two patched things up."

She nodded. "We're good. We've agreed to focus on our children's happiness first, and figure everything else out as we go." She held up his hand and kissed it. "And we agreed that you and I, are going to work on being you and I again. I hope you're okay with that decision."

He answered as if a weight had been lifted from his shoulders. "We're the three amigos! I'm the happiest man in the world."

They moved with the beat until the song ended, hearing Maddy call his name to approving applause of the audience. Adam walked out on stage, waving to the raucous sea of people. When he reached a mic, he shouted. "Viva Nueva Venezuela!"

The people cheered back in unison. "Viva Nueva Venezuela!"

It took the crowd some time to settle, but no one was in a hurry. When they did, Adam continued in English, still not yet fully fluent in Spanish. "The president wishes he could be here tonight, but with the current situation, we decided it best that he remain in a secure location."

The crowd chanted the president's name for a full minute. "Al-ve-rez! Al-ve-rez!"

When the cheering subsided, Adam continued. "Our nation is on a path to achieve great things with our economy, human rights and also our culture. That is why I'm proud to present a new award for the first time."

He held the golden medal hung beneath three cloth bands of yellow, blue and red representing the colors of the nation's flag. The throng clapped as the image was shown on the large screens on each side of the massive stage. "It is my pleasure to present the first Medalla Nacional de Artes Escénicas to international superstar, Madeline Blaze!"

The applause was thunderous as he pinned the medal onto her sexy green sequined costume. He grasped her hand and faced the crowd, raising it triumphantly. "Viva Nueva Venezuela!"

Once again, the crowd responded. "Viva Nueva Venezuela!" As he stood there marveling in the power of the moment, another sound broke the trance, sirens blaring over the stadium speaker. *Oh no! This can't be happening!* The sound of jet engines and machine gun fire erased the party atmosphere as everyone surged away from the stage and toward exits. Panic fueled by adrenaline gripped him. *What was I thinking!* With her hand still in his, he yanked. "We have to go!"

They reached Ens as the bullets from above ripped the stage, striking most of the band members as well as them. They fell in a heap as shouts and moans ricocheted from every direction. The memory of being shot by Liza ten years earlier flashed. He spoke as loud as he could, his breath short. "We'll be okay."

Finding his bearings, he saw blood flowing from Ensley's chest as she flailed, trying to stop the bleeding coming from Maddy's neck. He moved to help, repeating his promise. "We'll be okay."

Another jet sounded, seeming to be at a higher altitude. His arm motioned toward the armored vehicle. "We need to move."

A whistling noise he had only heard in movies filled the air as even more panic ensued. He felt the concussion of the bomb explosion, then the heat of the accompanying flames, which touched every part of his body. The blast flung him yards away. Impacting the ground everything went dark, and for the second time in the past two months, he felt as if he had died as blackness stole his consciousness.

When he awoke, Adam knew he had passed out, but had no idea for how long. The smell of burnt flesh filled his nose causing him to cough, sending powdery gray ash away from his mouth which was smashed against the ground. He was amazed. *I'm alive.*

His next thought was of Ensley and Maddy. He tried to get up and find them, before realizing part of the stage rigging had collapsed on the lower half of his body. *Damn.* He twisted and wiggled as the remaining flames of the explosion licked all around, making his breathing labored. He finally freed himself and relief swept over him as he saw Ensley and Maddy helping each other from beneath charred and splintered plywood, which had been the flooring of the stage.

He clambered over mangled metal to reach them. "You're both alive!"

He kissed Ensley's soot covered lips, and they never tasted so good, then he hugged Maddy. "We're all alive."

Maddy was the first to make the next observation. "And we're all naked. Our hair…and our clothes have been burned right off our bodies."

He started laughing at the absurdity of it all, then spied the mangled body of the drummer from the band. Realization of the certain death toll hit, and anger boiled up inside. "Santos is a dead man!"

Ens questioned. "What are you talking about?"

"The Brazilian President. He's the one who ordered this, and he's going to pay."

Another plane buzzed the wrecked stadium, and Maddy made a suggestion. "Let's get the hell out of here first. Seems he wants to take another shot at us."

Adam fumed. "That crazy psycho! This has to stop!"

He stood, helping the women to their feet, when he spied a CBN reporter and cameraman, and inspiration hit. "I've heard that son-of-a-bitch is superstitious. Follow my lead."

Walking with bare feet over a demolished and charred scene of death and destruction, their hairless bodies were covered only in a ghostly layer of ash and soot, bathed in moonlight. People moaned all around, and there were too many corpses too count. Looking like specters, Adam called to the reporter. "Hey! We've got your story right here."

With eyes as wide as hockey pucks, the reporter and cameraman scrambled toward them, delicately stepping around those who had perished in the massacre. The reporter spoke excitedly. "There are survivors!" Getting closer, he asked. "Who are you?"

Giving them time to get set, Adam waited, wanting to be sure his words were captured clearly.

When fully ready, the reporter asked again. "Who are you? How did you survive?"

The hand mic was pushed close, his blue eyes almost glowing, contrasting with the gray ash layer covering his body. "I'm Adam Clayborn."

The mic went to the left. "I'm Ensley Springer."

Then to the other woman. "And I'm the one and only Maddy Blaze, and someone blew up my fucking concert!"

Adam yanked the handheld mic away from the reporter as the cameraman pushed in for a close-up. He spoke slow and deliberately. "We've been to hell, and returned with a message for President Paulo Santos from Satan himself." Adam leaned closer, glaring into the lens like a crazed man. "End this invasion now, or he claims your soul this very night."

With that, he handed the mic back to the reporter and turned, walking away. Ens and Maddy followed as the reporter asked more questions. "How did you survive? What do you mean, you've been to hell?" When they didn't respond, the reporter stopped and faced the camera. "I don't know what we just witnessed, or exactly what they meant about going to hell, but I'm positive it will be replayed a thousand times."

Adam's ploy worked to perfection. Santos reversed course and ended the invasion. The death toll was just under ten-thousand, which was too many, but far less than it would have been if the invasion had not been stopped that night. A cleaned up, but bald Adam summed up his feelings the next day in a joint address to the nation with President Alverez. "Our nation has barely begun to show the world what we can do!" It was the proudest moment of his life.

CHAPTER FIFTY-ONE

Ensley held Adam's hand as a nurse wheeled her into a delivery room in Dr. Chavez's new Venezuelan facility. She felt reassured as he stroked her damp forehead, pushing away her short hair, still growing back from being singed off six months ago in the failed invasion attack. She attempted humor. "Maybe we can re-schedule? I'm not sure I'm ready for this."

He tried to comfort her, but the quiver in his voice seemed to betray his nerves. "You're doing great."

She gripped his hand tight as monitors indicated the onset of another contraction. "That's easy for you to say. Agh! This is a big one!"

Dr. Chavez strode into the sparkling white room dressed in her ubiquitous black scrubs. "I hope I didn't miss all the fun."

Ens fired back as she caught her breath. "You call this fun?"

Grinning, the doctor replied. "I guess that depends on who's asking and who's answering." She moved between Ensley's raised legs, assessing the situation. "Good, everything is progressing on schedule."

The monitors chirped as Ens began panting. "Maybe I should

have had that epidural after all. Another one's coming!"

"As it should. You'll be a mother very soon." Dr. Chavez spoke so calmly that she could have been talking about the weather on a sunny day, not the arrival of a new life into the world. She stared at Ens. "You need to ignore everyone and everything but me. Do you understand?"

"Yes." Two quick breaths later, she answered again. "Yes."

Chavez gave instruction. "Deep breaths until I say push. Not until then."

Sweat dripped from Ensley's forehead as she gasped for air. "Okay...okay."

As the baby's head began to crown, the doctor performed an episiotomy, then demanded action. "PUSH!"

A primal scream filled the room. "Ahhhhhh!"

Dr. Chavez's shoulders lowered. "The baby's head is through. Relax until the next contraction."

Adam offered encouragement. "Hang in there. You're doing great. It won't be long now!"

Ensley nodded as she caught her breath. Soon, her panting picked back up. "Another one's starting!"

Chavez made the awaited announcement. "One more good push should do it. Are you ready?"

Her answer came between gasps. "Yes...yes."

Dr. Chavez gave the order. "PUSH!"

Ens bore down. "Uhhhhh!"

Suddenly, they heard the doctor's excited voice. "He's here, Ensley. Your son is born!" She cleared his airway, then held up the newborn who made his own gasp, then cried. "He looks perfect." The doctor laid the waxy-white-coated infant on the new mother's chest, umbilical cord still attached. "Hold him. We're not quite finished."

Ensley touched her baby for the first time and wept freely. "I can't believe it. We have a baby."

Tears ran down Adam's face as he repeated her words. "We have a baby."

The nurse who had monitored the birth stepped forward with two clamps and placed them on the still attached cord. Dr. Chavez glanced at Adam and spoke playfully. "You have stood around long enough. Come do something useful."

"Me?"

"Of course. It's easy, just one swift snip."

Adam stepped forward and picked up the scissors, then snipped between the clamps, officially disconnecting child and mother.

Moving back in place, Chavez spoke calmly. "Give me one final push to deliver the placenta."

A determined sound followed. "Grrrrrrrr."

Dr. Chavez summed up the experience. "You did good, Ensley."

Shooting a glance at Adam, Dr. Chavez ribbed. "This is good practice for you, young man, I understand you'll be back here in a few days with Ms. Blaze."

Ensley watched as Adam blushed, then answered for him. "Our lives have been weird from the day we took our first breaths." She paused as she kissed her baby's head. "Why should this part be any different?"

CHAPTER FIFTY-TWO

Larry Knewell wanted the final show of his career to be spectacular, so he booked the three generations of participants in the Designer Baby storyline as his first guests. Two sofas were needed to seat the expanded family of Bree and Ansen, Zadie and Kade, with Adam positioned between Ensley and Maddy, who held babies in their arms. These individuals had changed history and he beamed as he kicked off the show. "Welcome to the final edition of *Rare Air*! You are the people who have had the most profound impact on our world, and this show. Thank you for joining me on this special night."

Bree spoke first. "With your continued interest in our evolving story, you've had an equally important role in helping the world understand human genetic modification. Thanks to your show, a large percentage of the public see us as real people, not as exaggerated caricatures. For that, I will be eternally grateful."

He blushed sincerely. "That's our goal on every broadcast. It's my responsibility to our viewers." Glancing down at his notes, he saw two names he would never forget and switched gears. "Before we go any farther, I want to pay tribute to two people who are no longer with us, but forever have a special place in my heart. Gwen and Ray lived lives that shown bright, and they were taken from us far too soon."

Maddy answered from the other end of the couch. "My mother was a great artist who always loved being on your show, even when you two were giving each other a hard time. And dad was a great scientist whose work paved the way for a cure to Huntington's Disease. I miss them every day."

The solemness of the moment was interrupted by the squirming of the child on Ensley's lap. Larry recognized the opportunity to transition back to happier news. "I think some introductions are in order." He pointed to Ensley. "Who's this little guy?"

The infant reached for his mother's coal black hair, almost completely regrown from the bombing they survived nearly a year ago. She calmed the child who had hair as black as hers, and the blue eyes and bigger build of his father. "This is Miles Clayborn, and he's three months old. It's already hard to remember what life was like before he arrived."

Not to seemingly be outdone, the child on Maddy's lap began wiggling. Larry turned to them. "And who is this sweet addition?"

Maddy's pale cheeks reddened as she wrangled the little girl, whose skin was as white as her own. Like her half-brother, she inherited her father's blue eyes. "I would like you to meet Gwena Blaze. She's named after her grandmother."

"That's precious." He smiled and glanced upward. "I'm sure your mother would approve." His eyes now dipped to his notes page again. "Speaking of mothers, I don't think you and Ensley experienced the same accelerated pregnancies as your mothers. Why is that?"

The shoulder shrug was immediate. "We have no idea. The children are developing at the same rapid pace the three of us did, but both Ens and I went the full nine-months. Seems we're still learning some secrets from the one and only, Dr. Cielo Chavez."

"Fascinating." With the children introduced, Larry turned to the man between them and teased. "So, Adam. Anything interesting going on in your life?"

Turning to peek at each child, he answered with a grin. "You could say I've been a little busy."

Larry asked the obvious question on millions of people's minds. "How are things working out for the three of you...I mean the five of you?"

All three smiled, with no hint of tension or animosity, as Adam took the first shot at answering. "I'll not get into the details of how we ended up here, but only talk about how we're proceeding. All three of us are one-hundred percent invested in doing what's best for these children. I'm living full time in New Venezuela while Ensley and Maddy are splitting their time between there and in the US. When they are down there Ensley and Miles stay with me, and Maddy's home is in the same neighborhood I live, making things easier for everyone."

Ensley took over. "As most people know, Adam and I were married for a while. While we're not ready to take the step of making it official again, our relationship is certainly close."

Without missing a beat, Maddy chimed in. "Us three have been best friends since the day we were born, and we're committed to each other in an unbreakable way. We'll always be the three amigos, best friends for life."

With the personal update for the younger set, Larry shifted attention back to the older generation. "Ansen, I was shocked and saddened to hear of your near fatal injury. I understand we almost lost you. How are things going in your rehabilitation?"

Ansen moved his leg as he sat on the non-descript cream colored sofa. "I'm a lucky man, Larry. My spinal cord was injured, but not severed. With intense physical therapy, I've regained a lot of mobility. I can even walk short distances with the aid of two special canes."

Nodding, Larry offered encouragement. "With your attitude and work ethic, I'm sure you'll be back to full strength soon."

Looking toward Ensley, Ansen gave an update that all of the guests knew and completely understood, but was heard by Larry a different way. "When something like this happens, it's natural to reassess some things in one's life. I've decided to permanently step back from some of my business and charity activities. Ensley has been filling in during my recuperation, and has agreed to step in full time in some of those roles."

Larry turned toward Ensley. "With your experience on the global stage advocating for GM rights, I have no doubt you'll be successful."

Her smile was innocent with no hint of the magnitude of her new title as the newly elected Matriarch of the Tree of Life Society. "It will keep me busy, but I have wise council on all major decisions."

Following up, Larry asked about her current job. "Will that lessen your time as Director of the Twenty-Three Chromosomes Foundation?"

"Fortunately, there is good news there as well. After the global condemnation of the attempted second invasion of New Venezuela, WAGE has lowered their level of vitriol against GM people. The current leader, Lesedi Khomalo, has resigned from her post to spend more time with her family. Over time, even our former enemies have changed their views. We've even heard from the original WAGE founders, and they are considering moving to New Venezuela. They say they like the inclusive culture being built there."

Larry was shocked. "You can't be talking about Becky Brown and Kelley Slaughter?"

A tilt of her head signaled the same type of disbelief. "The very same. In talking with them, they seem like changed women. I met them years before and could never have imagined that we would be inviting them to stay with us when they visit South America."

Shaking his head, he still couldn't believe what he was hearing. "Wow. You'll have to take a group photo and send it to me. I'll need proof to fully trust you on that."

Keeping the conversation moving, Larry turned his attention to Zadie and Kade. "Most everyone else here has been in the news lately, except for you two. What have you been up to lately?"

Answering for the couple, Zadie took the same tack as Ansen. She answered truthfully, but was heard one way by Larry but another by everyone else in the group. They understood the deeper meaning. "I've been involved with some of Ansen's businesses for a while, so now I'm one of the people advising Ensley in her new role. We're quite proud of her leadership skills."

Kade added additional information about a new phase of their life as he pointed to Miles and Gwena. "As new grandparents, we're scaling back on other parts of our business life and finding ways to help Ens and Maddy take care of those two wonderful children. We love those young women, and like most parents, want to help them succeed any way we can."

"Speaking of these young women, what's next for you, Maddy?"

Her knees bounced, keeping Gwena content as she replied. "I've been writing new material. With all the time I've spent in South America lately, I've had some new influences. It's been exciting and I've been inspired. I think my fans are going to like the Latin vibes on my next album."

"I can't wait to hear it." With that, Larry had one final update to get. "Adam, tell us the latest from New Venezuela. That country has seen so much change, it's incredible."

His eyes lit as he talked. "Incredible is a good word. Thanks to my contacts in the banking world, investment funds have flowed in, raising the living standards for all segments of the population. And working with President Alverez has been a delight. He's smart and has a unique connection to the people. Together, we've accomplished so much in so little time."

Larry's eyes narrowed as he pressed. "But to be fair, he had little choice in this partnership, right? You and the Anywhere Solutions army staged a violent takeover of the country."

"That's not *exactly* what happened." Adam's demeanor never changed as he tried to explain from his point of view. "General Rolan Volkov was the one who conceived and led the invasion with the goal of installing himself as the new leader. I happened to be in a position to turn power over to the leader of the opposition when former President Rojas was exiled to Cuba, and Volkov's men turned against him."

"But let's be clear, you were...*are* part of that army. In fact, you are the current Secretary of Defense."

Adam sighed. "I was in a dicey situation and aimed for the best outcome, and so far, things are headed the right way. The standard of living is up, access to healthcare is up, and free elections are schedule for next year. Even the surrounding countries seem happy. All of them have signed non-aggression *and* economic development pacts with us. They see what we are accomplishing and want to share in the growth. We're not only changing the country, we're changing the continent."

Larry chuckled. "And Brazil tossed President Santos out of office. How did it feel when you heard that news?"

Adam's smile widened. "He murdered thousands, and nearly killed us three. You saw the video. How do you think I felt?"

"I would say vindicated." Larry asked his final question. "I've reported on all of your lives for a long time, and this seems to be the happiest I've ever seen you...all of you. Am I right?"

Bree answered for her and Ansen. "For the two of us, absolutely. We're closer than we've ever been, and so proud of these accomplished young adults." Her face brightened. "And we're grand-parents! What's not to like!"

Zadie followed. "I could never have dreamed this would be how our lives would have turned out, but through it all, we couldn't be happier. And I'm with Bree, nothing beats being grandparents!"

Maddy was next in line. "I miss my parents more than I can put into words." She wiped the corners of her eyes. "But there's not a damned thing I can do about that other than to celebrate their lives, and I try to do that every day." She kissed the top of Gwena's head. "And now I have the most precious child ever, and a rockin career. It doesn't get much better."

Ensley swayed as Miles' eyes took long blinks, on the crest of falling asleep. "My career has never been more exciting, Adam and I are reconnecting, and we've been blessed with this sweet baby. Life is good. Very good."

"And you, Adam?"

He paused for a moment, as if gathering disparate thoughts. "I feel like I am exactly where I'm supposed to be. It seems like every experience, the good, the bad, and the ugly have been to prepare me for this moment in time. First of all, I love being a father, and I now have a new appreciation and respect for mine." He took a breath. "I'm also using my education, my business experience and the life lessons I've learned along the way to make a real difference in millions of people's lives. It feels like this is what I was made to do."

Larry looked into camera one as he wrapped this segment of his farewell show. "It has been an honor and, in some ways, a duty to cover what many call the biggest news story in history. Genetic modification of humans has been hailed as the crowning achievement of our species or alternately, the first step in changing the very definition of humanity itself. While I have had a front row seat, I offer no final judgment of where the truth may lay."

He turned to camera two. "What I can say is that I have been blessed to meet, and get to know some of the remarkable people at the epicenter of the story. I met three incredible women whose very lives were targeted because they dared carry the first GM babies to term. I witnessed them, along with their husbands, raise those remarkable children who have now become responsible adults."

Turning his gaze to slowly land on each of them, he continued. "Whatever your views may be on the wisdom of tinkering with our genome, no one can dispute that these individuals have changed the path of world history. Our air and water are cleaner due to their efforts, there is significantly less sickness and disease in the world, and the standard of living for millions has been raised. Now, human rights are being expanded in new and important ways."

Looking straight into the living rooms of his vast audience, Larry wrapped the segment. "While I am retiring, and ending my coverage of this story, I know that we are only at the end of the beginning of the saga. Who can guess the changes that Miles and Gwena will usher in during their lifetime? I certainly can't, but I know that I will be watching as a spectator and hoping for the best for them, and for humanity."

Larry addressed them one last time. "Thank you all for allowing me to share your stories with the world. It has been a blessing and a privilege." He turned back to camera one. "And most of all, thanks to all of you for inviting me into your homes every night. You're the best."

As the consummate professional, he had kept his emotions in check, but his feelings of gratitude found their way onscreen as his voice cracked. "For one last time, thank you all for tuning in to *Rare Air*."

∞

Dr. Chavez sat in her darkened office watching Larry Knewell's final episode as she sipped fine Kentucky bourbon. She laughed as he signed off. "We'll see if you can stay retired when you see what comes next. Adam leads an army and Ensley is the Matriarch of the Tree of Life Society. Just think of what that power couple might do. And Maddy, she has been the outlier all along, but is a truly great ambassador for the GM movement. Working together, that trio is to be reckoned with."

She took another sip. "Then there is the next generation. Wait until Larry and the world see what Miles and Gwena will do. They will make a bigger splash than all the others combined!" She raised her glass toward the television. "Here's to you, Larry Knewell. You've done your job well."

THE END

Thank you for reading *Designer Babies Volume Three, Passing the Torch*. If you liked the book, I would be grateful if you would consider putting up some stars on the Amazon store page. Even better, if you have time, I'd appreciate a review. They are the life blood of independent authors, and your review would have a huge impact on my book's visibility to other readers.

DAVID WITT